MOON

MAGGIE
SHAYNE

Originally Published 2001 by Spilled Candy Books

http://www.MaggieShayne.com

Ebook and Cover Formatted by Jessica Lewis
http://AuthorsLifeSaver.com

Created with Vellum

CHAPTER 1

Mirabella lifted her head, blinked her sleepy eyes, and found herself standing upright, bound to the pole at her back. She couldn't move. It was only as she tried that she realized her body was entwined by rough, fraying rope that twisted around and around her from her ankles to her shoulders. When she pulled against it, it seemed to grow even tighter, cutting more deeply into her flesh, until her legs and arms tingled. She went still and waited for the pain to subside, the blood to flow into her limbs once more. A chill wind whipped her hair and drew goose bumps to her flesh.

The sky was a series of brushstrokes in varying shades of grim. Black as coal up high, then a stripe of wet slate, and a slash of bruise purple. Lower still, the horizon lightened to a pearly gray haze. No stars. No moon. Somewhere beyond the horizon, the sun struggled to rise while the darkness conspired to keep it down. But the light won out, as it always does.

Bit by bit, the area around her became visible. Though the entire place was shrouded in creeping, silver mists, she managed to strain enough to see. Herself first. Her body. With her head cocked downward at a sharp angle she saw that the garment she wore beneath the serpentine rope, was ragged. Barely more than a burlap sack with holes torn for her head and arms to poke through.

Sackcloth...?

Her legs and feet were bare. She stood on an upturned wooden crate, and below it, around it, were mounds of brush, limbs, twigs, branches. Something was smudged over the skin of her legs and arms. Soot or ashes or....

Sackcloth and ashes....

Something acrid hung in the air. A familiar scent she ought to know.

Gasoline?

She sucked in a breath, and it seemed the wind died all at once. Her hair fell down to shield her eyes, raven strands, uncombed and wild. Then slowly, she lifted her head upright again, squinting to see what was going on around her.

People. A crowd of them stood elbow to elbow, staring at her. Somber, oddly quiet, their faces grim. She blinked and realized she was in the park in the center of town. She made out familiar landmarks. The Ezra Town Hall was just beyond the crowd to her right, its white paint chipping, hand-tooled sign swinging when the breeze picked up again. The road lay behind her. She heard a car going past but couldn't see it. To her left, the river tumbled by, oblivious to her plight She could hear it tripping over stones and laughing at its own clumsiness. And in between, people. So many people.

Their stares were cold, she thought as her gaze skimmed them all. Then all at once, her attention was caught, riveted like a fly on flypaper, to one man. He looked more hostile than any of the others. His dark eyes stared right back at her, piercing her soul with their anger and condemnation. He stood directly in front of her, and he held her eyes with his.

His jaw was clenched and hard. His hostility reached her in waves so potent she felt them like physical blows.

I'd kill you myself if I could!

She felt the words in her mind, very clearly, though he hadn't opened his mouth to speak them. God, what had she done to so infuriate that man?

She wanted to cry out but couldn't. She tried, but no sound emerged. As if fear had frozen her very breath, robbed her of her voice. She wanted to move, but the ropes held on too tightly for that. She could only move her head, and she did, swinging it from side to side, seeking help in that crowd of onlookers. But no one there would help her. And her desperate gaze returned again and again to that angry man in the front. Everyone else faded to background colors. He alone remained clear, vivid. His emotions. His hatred. As clear to her as her own name.

"Mirabella St. Angeline," came a disembodied voice. "You have been found guilty by a duly appointed court of the crime of teaching Witchcraft to a minor and contributing to her mental illness and subsequent suicide. For these crimes, you have been sentenced to death by fire to be carried out this day at dawn. Do you have any last words?"

She searched the air for the source of that voice, but found no speaker. She tried to say something in her own defense, tried to shout her denial, tried to plead, to beg for her life. Her mouth moved, but no sound emerged. And the man in the front took a step closer, his fists clenched, tears standing unshed in his eyes, and he said, "Burn in hell, Witch. Burn in hell for what you did to my daughter!"

"May God have mercy on your soul," the other voice intoned.

She heard the flames even before she saw them. The snapping jaws and smacking lips of hungry fire catching sight of its next meal. Panic gripped her in hands of ice when she saw the people in the crowd, bearing torches now. Where they got them, she didn't know. They'd had none a moment ago. But now they had come to life, those somber, silent onlookers. Shouting, swearing, cursing her, they surged forward, hurling their torches and their hatred at her.

The flames spread, licking up the gasoline and following it around her in a perfect circle. And then they leapt higher, so high they blotted out everything else, a towering monster that gobbled its way closer. Merciless heat seared her face. And yet, cruelly, almost teasingly, the curtain of fire parted and closed again and again, giving her glimpses of the man. His eyes were still affixed to hers. She felt her skin roasting, blistering and peeling. Her blood boiled and hissed as it bubbled from her pores. Her flesh melted and fell away from her bones. Pain: she didn't feel it, she became it. The embodiment of burning, screaming torment. She wished for death. But death did not come.

The ropes that held her burned through, and she stumbled from the crate, a human torch, twisting and writhing through the pyre, kicking aside piles of burning brush, until she came to the area beyond it. And still she staggered forward, until she slammed bodily into the solid chest of the hateful man. Her hands twisted into the fabric of his shirt as she pled in silence for his help. For his mercy. And then his shirt caught fire as well. She could still see his face, his hard, cold eyes staring into hers through a fiery veil. Then the fabric tore, and she fell to the ground, and he fell with her. She was tangled in him, in his burning arms and legs, and the dancing flames. His mouth found hers, and he kissed her as they burned.

Gasping, her mouth wide with anguish and silent screams, Mirabella opened her eyes. She was not on fire. She was on her bedroom floor, the curtains from her window twisted around her body, the rod bent almost in half and lying across her legs. She closed one hand in her own hair, as she panted for breath, whispering "Oh, God, oh, God," over and over again. Her heart was pounding so hard it thrummed in her ears. She was burning up with an inexplicable fever and damp with sweat.

She tried to stand, shaking so hard she fell to her knees again, then managed to get up and stay there on the second try. She got untangled from the curtains, dropping the rod, dragging herself to her bathroom, and stepping into the shower even as she cranked on the knobs. She didn't even undress first. Just stepped into the too cold water and let it sooth the imaginary burns she could still feel. Cool the fever that had no physical cause.

The water soaked her, soaked her nightgown, chilled her skin. She braced her arms against the wall to hold herself up and turned her face into the flow. And finally, when she felt as if she was breathing again and those phantom flames had been extinguished, she turned the water off.

She had never even tugged the shower curtain closed, she thought vaguely, lifting her head. From the corner of her eye, she caught a glimpse of her own reflection in the mirror on the other side of the small bathroom. Hair tangled and dripping, face flushed and wet. She turned to face the mirror fully...

...and went utterly still. A woman stood behind her in the mirror. A woman with auburn hair and deep blue eyes.

Mirabella spun around, her heart in her throat. But no one was there.

Heart racing, she kept looking from the mirror, to the shower stall again and again, as she clambered out, grappled for a towel. She was shaking all over. "What the hell was that? What the hell...?"

Fighting to catch her breath, calm her heart, she knew only two things, and she knew them with vivid clarity.

Whatever had just happened to her had not been a mere dream.

And she was fully awake now.

"JUST WHAT DO you think you're doing. Rowan?"

Jonathon Hawthorne stood in the open doorway of his daughter's bedroom, his breath knocked out of him by what he saw. She sat in the middle of her floor, surrounded by a ring of candles, which were the only light in the room. Her legs were crossed, eyes closed. Some tribal drumbeat pattered from her stereo system. She didn't open her eyes or react to his presence in any way, beyond the slight stiffening of her limbs.

"Damn it. Rowan, what have I told you about this garbage?" He strode into the room, hit the light switch first, the power button on the stereo second.

When he looked at her again, her eyes were open and furious.

For just a second he could have sworn he was looking at her mother. She used to get that same infuriated, offended, and slightly arrogant expression when he dismissed her farfetched beliefs as nonsense.

Unfortunately, he'd been right. Otherwise, Ashley would still be alive. And he was damned if he would stand by and watch Rowan start down the same delusional path her mother had traveled

"Since when do you just walk into my room?" Rowan asked without getting up.

"Since I don't want my house to go up in flames. Put the damn candles out. Rowan."

"You're supposed to knock!"

"I *did* knock. You apparently thought it was part of the infernal pounding on that CD you had playing."

"That was ritual drumming by a group of Native Holy Men. *Not* infernal pounding."

He pushed a hand through his hair. Rowan was everything to him. A mirror image of her mother, who had been everything to him, too. He just looked at her for a moment. At her deep burnished hair, endlessly long and perfectly straight; at her smooth, ivory skin; at her thick, dark lashes that didn't need the enhancement of mascara in the least. Fourteen. Five-three. A perfect size two with a burgeoning figure he pretended not to notice. Not a little girl any more. A young woman. And he felt sorry for the men she would encounter in a few more years. She'd put them all on their knees without even trying.

Lately, Rowan had been pulling away from him. And he hated it, but didn't have a clue how to fix things. Damn Ashley for leaving him to raise their daughter alone. *She* would know what to do with a daughter who suddenly changed from a smiling dimpled little girl into a brooding, incommunicative young woman who dressed mostly in black and rarely spoke more than a sentence at a time to her parent.

She sat now, glowering as she used a gold plated snuffer to extinguish her candles one by one, not even looking at him. "So what's the big emergency, Dad?" she asked when she'd snuffed the last one.

"I...nothing. I just wondered if you wanted a ride to school."

She stared at him lips thinning.

"Do you?"

"No. Anything else?"

He sighed. "Rowan, what were you doing in here, just now? With the candles and the drumming and-"

For the first lime, a hint of a smile tugged at her lips. "I was talking to Mom. Or trying to, at least."

It brought him up short. Like a punch in the gut, it drove the breath out of him, and it took him a minute to get it back. He closed his eyes, shook his head slowly, and when he could get words out again, he said, "Honey, your mother is dead. You can't talk to her, and anyone who tells you otherwise is a con-artist and a liar."

Her huge, expressive eyes grew angry again. "Just because you don't believe in something doesn't mean it doesn't exist!"

He opened his mouth to shout back at her but closed it again. "Okay. I don't want to fight with you about this. Breakfast is on the table. Come downstairs and eat before you leave for school. All right?"

She pursed her lips. "Yeah. Whatever."

"Ten minutes."

He left her, closing the door behind him, then pausing in the hall to ask himself if he was doing anything right in any way, shape or form, where she was concerned. He'd read all the books out there for single dads raising daughters on their own. God knew there were enough of them. He'd listened to all the experts, and he was still lost as to how to deal with the sudden, drastic changes in his daughter.

Downstairs in the sunny, mostly glass breakfast nook, he picked up the newspaper, sampled his oatmeal and waited for Rowan to show up, determined to have a non-confrontational conversation with her for once.

But the story that caught his attention did nothing to help along those lines. Another crime with "occult" stamped all over it had taken place overnight. Someone had butchered a house cat in the local cemetery and painted odd symbols on a headstone in its blood. It was the fifth pet to have been killed in an apparent ritual sacrifice this month. One of the kids being questioned, the story said, had been seen running from the cemetery when police arrived. No doubt, the full details would be waiting on his desk when he arrived at work. Poor goddamned cat, he thought.

And he was supposed to allow his daughter to start poking around in this kind of bullshit? Incense and candles and spells and charms? No way. Not in this lifetime.

Rowan came into the breakfast nook. She wore a heavy chain around her neck and a choker made of leather. Burgundy lipstick, purple eyeliner, black tank top, and jeans.

Sighing, he laid the paper down. "Honey, what's wrong?"

She looked at him as if startled, her eyes the biggest, bluest eyes in the universe. She had unusually large pupils. It was common, he'd heard, in fair skinned, blue-eyed girls. But he didn't think anything about her was common.

"What makes you think somewthing's wrong?" she asked.

"I don't know. You just seem to be going through some changes lately, and...well, it concerns me."

"It's called growing up, Dad." She put her attention back on her oatmeal.

"Is there anything you want to talk to me about? Anything going on at school or-?"

She met his eyes, her own looking impatient now. "I'm not taking drugs or having sex if that's what you're asking."

He felt his jaw drop. "No. That's not what I was asking," he stammered. "You're way too young for me to be worrying about those kinds of things."

She rolled her eyes. "Right."

"What's that supposed to mean?"

"Nothing, Dad. I gotta go. Tell the people on your happy little planet I said bye, will you?" She softened the words with a teasing wink.

"Very funny."

Rowan got to her feel and slung her backpack over her

shoulder. She started to go, then sighed and turned back. "Actually, there is something I want to talk about," she said.

He almost grinned. She wanted to talk to him! Finally! He smothered the urge to smile ear to ear, put on a serious face, and said. "What is it?"

She drew a deep breath, as if for courage. "Mom. I want to know everything about her."

"But honey. I've always talked to you about your mom. I think I've probably told you just about everything I know."

"No, you haven't," she said.

He held her gaze for only a moment. And then he had to look away. Shit. How much did she know?

When he looked at her again, her eyes were closed. "I see her in my dreams, you know. Especially lately. She was so beautiful...way more than she is in any of her pictures. I don't remember her being that beautiful."

"You were only four, honey. Don't feel bad for not remembering. And if you wonder how beautiful your mom was, all you have to do is look in a mirror."

She opened her eyes. They were damp. "Really? You think I look like her?"

"More every day." He was getting a little tight in the throat himself.

Rowan licked her lips. "Dad, it's like she's trying to tell me something, but I just can't get what. That's why I've been trying to talk to her, when I'm awake, you know, but...well, so far, I don't think it's working."

He swallowed the dryness in his throat. "That's because it's not possible. I'm sorry, hon, but it's just not."

"I don't believe that. And I don't think Mom did, either."

She leaned down, and kissed his cheek. "But I'm going to be late if I don't get going. Sometime, though, Dad, you have to tell me about Mom. The stuff you haven't told me before. Okay?"

"Yeah. Sure." He said it softly, distracted, shaken. His daughter managed a smile, but he thought he saw doubt in her eyes. "I promise," he added.

"Okay," she said. She reached behind her to pull her Ipod out of her backpack and push her earbuds into place.

He watched her go and made a mental note to call the school, set up conferences with some of Rowan's teachers. Maybe that would give him some insight into what was going on with her. There was that one teacher she was always talking about...Miss Saint A., Rowan called her. She was one of the only teachers his daughter ever mentioned in any positive sort of way.

Yes. Miss Saint A. He'd start with her. She might be just the person to help him wipe all this hocus-pocus nonsense out of Rowan's head once and for all.

CHAPTER 2

"I have to say, I agree with you, Mirabella. I don't think it was a dream either."

"What then?"

Mirabella sat across from her dearest friend. Gwenyth, at a round table in the back of Gwen's shop. Between them, Tarot cards lay face up, spread out in familiar patterns. The shop was housed in the lower front portion of the oversized Victorian house Gwen had inherited from her great-grandmother. She lived in the rest of it. Along with whatever stray creatures wandered in looking for a place to rest or a solid meal. Gwen could never turn away an animal in need.

The front of the shop had a large bay window that housed hunks of uncut quartz and amethyst, an assortment of candle holders and incense burners, several pieces of pyrite from the stream out back, a stack of obscure looking books, and a black cat called Circe who was usually curled up, sound asleep. Circe was the first and the favorite of all Gwen's pets. The gold, gothic lettering on the door spelled *Gwenyth's Chamber* in a curving arch. Beneath it, in smaller block letters, was a list:

. . .

Occult Supplies

Tools of Divination

Herbs

Oils

Brews

Candles

Psychic Readings

by appointment only

The shop-and Gwenyth-fit into this small town about as well as a square peg in a round hole. Mirabella had always been much more discreet about her beliefs. She had to be. She was a teacher at the high school, for goodness sake!

"If it wasn't a dream, Gwen, then what was it?" she asked.

Gwen drew a deep breath and flipped over another Tarot card. She was a petite woman, with honey gold hair that curled untamed to her shoulders. She wore jeans and a black sweatshirt that said "Witch and famous" on the front in orange letters. And of course, there was the ever-present pentacle on a chain around her neck.

"A warning," she said at last. "I think it was a warning. It's definitely not past life, though there are connections to one. It looks like...something in the future." She looked up from the cards, meeting Mirabella's eyes, and hers seemed worried. "Honey, have you been talking to any of your students about the Craft?"

"You think I'm insane? Of course not."

Gwen shrugged. "Well. I don't know then. You know, up until recently, Wiccans in Ezra Township have been left pretty much alone. The locals grate their teeth and roll their eyes and tolerate us. Barely. But the tide's shifting, Mirabella. It's getting dangerous out there."

Bella nodded. "I know."

"Maybe you don't."

Frowning, Mirabella said, "What do you mean?"

Gwen licked her lips nervously, and Bella could see she was debating whether to say anything more. Then she seemed to decide all at once. "I've been getting threats."

Mirabella sucked in a breath and widened her eyes. "What kinds of threats?"

Gwen got up from her seat at the table and walked past the row of pewter figurines to step behind the counter with the antique register on it. She drew a manila envelope from beneath the counter and slid it across to Mirabella. Bella opened it and took out the contents. Scraps of paper, entire sheets, some folded, some not. All basically bearing the same message. "We don't want Witches in Ezra Township. Get out while you still can." Some were more colorfully worded than others, but the gist was the same.

"How long has this been going on?" Mirabella asked.

"A couple of weeks. About as long as the spree of animal murders they've been attributing to this so-called occult group that's cropped up. The problem is, there is no occult group. I'm pretty well networked, and I'd know if there was. I haven't heard a thing. Either these nuts are from out of town or...or I don't know what to think."

"Why didn't you say something about these threats before, Gwen?"

She shrugged. "Didn't see what good it would have done." She licked her lips. "I've had an offer on the house, Bella. Mark Hayes from the real estate office is willing to give me a very good price for it."

"When did you go see him?" Bella asked, frowning.

"I didn't. He came to see me. Actually, it had nothing to do with business. He asked permission to do some fishing in the stream out back-way back in April, and he's been popping in ever since. Says he's fallen in love with the place."

"But...you're not considering selling?"

Gwen shrugged. "I wasn't. But since all of this—yeah, I'm thinking about taking it."

"That's totally unlike you, Gwen. To give up and run away."

Gwen licked her lips. "I don't like the whole town thinking I'm into butchering innocent house pets and defacing hallowed ground in the cemetery."

"Nobody thinks that!" Mirabella shouted.

Gwen tilted her head to one side, frowning at Bella as if she were sprouting horns. "Honey, of course they think that! Who else are they gonna suspect? I'm the only Witch in town, so far as most people know. Everyone else is pretty much in the broom closet. To the locals, it's the natural conclusion."

The chimes over the door jangled, and both women turned around to see Billy Cantone, a man they'd both gone to high school with, coming toward them. He was wearing his uniform, star pinned to his chest, right over his heart. And he wasn't smiling.

"Well, hello Billy," Gwen said. "Dare I hope you're looking for a love potion or a good luck charm?"

He pursed his lips. "Fraid not. Gwen. This is official business." He nodded at Mirabella. "Surprised to see you here, Bella."

"Shoot, Bella and I are old friends, Billy. We see each other quite often," Gwen said before Bella could say a word. Then she turned to Bella again. "I'm sorry I couldn't be of help to you. I know as a teacher you're as concerned as I am about this rash of nastiness hitting our town, but I really don't have a clue who's behind it."

She was giving her an out. Letting her keep her "cover" intact. Mirabella lowered her head and muttered her good-byes. When what she wanted to do was look Billy in the eye and tell him the truth.

"You'd better go. Bella." Gwen said, glancing at her watch. "You hang around here any longer you may just lose your job." Then she tapped the watch. "You know how Sally Hayes hates her teachers showing up late."

"Yeah, well, she might forgive me if I tell her I was at her husband's favorite fishing hole. But you're right." She got the message loud and clear. She risked her job every time she came into this shop and would lose it for sure if she spoke her mind to Billy. Still, she was ashamed of herself as she turned and walked away.

But as it turned out, she didn't get all that far.

ROWAN WAS deep in thought as she walked to school, and she shut the world out in her usual way—with her Ipod blasting and her earbuds firmly in place. Her body was changing. Her mind was changing. And things were...happening to her that she didn't understand. Her father didn't want to talk about it. Seemed almost afraid of it. But Rowan knew somehow, way down deep, that her mother would have understood. That she had gone through these very same things. That she'd had...something extra.

Just like Rowan had.

Reaching into her jacket pocket, Rowan fingered the small woven pouch she'd found tucked away in the attic with her mother's things. The things inside it meant something. She just didn't know what.

She heaved a sigh as she turned to cross West Main in the usual place, walking on autopilot, because she knew the way by heart. She'd been walking it for a long time now. As she crossed, she glanced at the shop across the street. *Gwenyth's Chamber*. She'd been in there a few times, even picked up a couple of books. But when she'd worked up the courage to ask the owner a few, tentative questions, the little blond had given her a sad smile and told her to come back when she was eighteen.

How was she supposed to understand what was happening to her if no one would even discuss it?

As she watched, Officer Cantone walked into the shop, and a second later, a woman walked out. Rowan frowned and looked closer. That was Miss Saint A, her homeroom teacher! Coming out of that kind of a shop? But...did that mean that she....

Before she could complete the thought, Miss Saint A looked right at her, shouted something, and raced toward her. Startled. Rowan yanked off her headphones and glanced to her left. At first, she saw nothing, but in a split second, a truck careened around the sharp curve and was bearing down on her. And for just an instant, she was frozen in panic.

Then Miss Saint A's body crashed into hers, and the impact hurled her out of the way. The two of them hit the pavement together in one big tangle. The landing hurt like hell-and Rowan had landed on top!

BELLA WASN'T sure what happened. She came out of Gwen's shop and looked up to see a woman.

And then she froze, because it was the same women she'd glimpsed in her bathroom mirror this morning!

The woman lifted a hand and pointed.

"Who are you? What the hell do you want with me?"

But the woman shook her head harshly and jabbed her finger again and again toward the road. Bella turned to look, she saw the girl in the road, and in a flash, she knew the truck, was coming. Before she saw it, before she heard it, she knew it. She shouted a warning and ran.

The truck came thundering then, and the girl seemed frozen in fear. Bella's body crashed into hers, and her momentum carried them both to the roadside, to the pavement, hitting hard. The girl's breath burst from her lungs with an "unh!" when they landed.

Tires squealed and Bella smelled burning rubber even before she turned to see the smoke rolling off the wheels as the truck came to a stop a block down, cockeyed in the road.

She got to her feet, helping the girl up as well. For the first time, she realized it was one of her own students. Rowan Hawthorne.

Often introspective and always questioning authority. Bella liked her. She brushed the dust from the girl's leather jacket and looked her up and down. "Are you all right, Rowan?"

Rowan nodded, looking dazedly at the truck, then back at Bella again. "That jerk almost killed me," she said, straightening her skirt with an angry tug. Then she glanced at Bella more closely, her eyes narrowing. "Your lip is bleeding, Miss Saint A. Are you all right?"

"I'm fine." She touched her lip, drew her fingers away, and looked at the blood.

But Rowan's eyes were even narrower now. "God, look at your head."

Bella touched the spot where her head hurt, sucked in a breath, and drew her fingers away. A lump seemed to be forming already, and it hurt like hell. People were coming toward them now from the shops on either side of the street.

"I didn't see that truck," Rowan said. "You yelled, and then he was just there. How did you know?"

"My God, my God, Rowan! Are you two all right?" The deep, male voice was accompanied by pounding footfalls as a man raced toward them.

Even as Rowan called, "I'm fine, Dad." Mirabella turned to look his way. And the moment she saw his face, her blood rushed to her feet so fast she felt dizzy. Her vision swam, and she pressed a hand to her forehead automatically and closed her eyes.

He was beside them in a heartbeat, grabbing hold of her shoulders. "Hold on. Easy now. I've got you."

Gentle hands eased her down onto the sidewalk. Tender fingers pushed her hair aside. "Ah, you've got a nasty bump here. Maybe a slight concussion."

"I'm sure it's nothing like that." She opened her eyes again, hoping with everything in her that it had been a trick or a hallucination-that he would look totally different now.

But her wish was not granted. He was hunkering near her, his hands on her face, his eyes filled with concern and questions, not hate and rage. But he was the same. Dark hair, dark eyes. A face as hard and square as if it were a bust caned in marble.

The man from her dream. And that meant the girl whose death Mirabella had somehow caused-had to be Rowan.

Bella looked at her. Young and stunningly beautiful, sitting beside her looking worried. Suicide. God, no. The very thought made Bella's eyes fill with tears.

"She saved my life, Dad. Did you see it?"

"I saw," he said, and he frowned just a little at his daughter and reached out to pick up the fallen headphones. "Maybe these ought to come off when you're crossing streets, hmm?"

She shrugged sheepishly, and he smiled, then pulled her

close for a gentle hug. "Are you sure you're okay, hon? God, if anything ever happened to you, I think I'd lose my mind."

"Dad, you're so melodramatic." Rowan said, but she hugged him back.

When he released her, he turned to Bella again. "Let me take you to the clinic, have that bump looked at."

Several of Bella's colleagues were gathered around them now, and Gwen and Officer Billy Cantone were coming toward them. Almost all the teachers who lived in town walked this route to school. Often they would meet in Granny Kate's Coffee Shop, a few doors away from Gwen's place, for a fresh baked doughnut and a hot mug of brew before heading to work. No one in town was quite as well loved as Granny Kate.

"I'm fine, really," Bella said. She sought Gwen's eyes and repeated it. "Just a close call. I'm really okay." Gwen nodded, licking her lips and backing off. Bella knew she was trying to protect her. With so many colleagues around, she didn't want to publicize their friendship. Officer Billy was already heading away to talk to the truck driver.

Bella started to get up to prove she was okay, only to have the man clasp her shoulders in his big hands and help her to her feet. "That bump doesn't look like something to be ignored," he said. His voice did things to her. She felt its reverberations echoing in her belly and in her throat.

"I really have to get to school." Did she sound a little breathless? He was standing too close, and his hands were still on her shoulders, and his eyes were all over her.

"School?" His brows rose, thick dark arches. "You're one of Rowan's teachers, aren't you?"

She nodded. "Mirabella Saint Angeline, Freshman English." she said.

"It's Miss Saint A, Dad. I've told you about her before." Rowan looked curiously from one of them to the other.

He nodded, not taking his eyes off Mirabella. "Odd, I was just thinking of you this morning." And when she only frowned at him in confusion, he said. "I'm Jonathon," he said, "Jonathon Hawthorne. Rowan's father."

That much, she'd gathered on her own.

"I really think you ought to let Dad take you to that clinic, Miss Saint A." Rowan said. "You don't look too good. And I feel guilty enough already."

"You shouldn't feel guilty at all, Rowan."

"I won't-once I know for sure you didn't give yourself brain damage knocking me out from in front of that truck."

Mirabella lowered her head. Tough to argue with that.

Someone reached out to hand Mirabella her soft-sided briefcase. Bella followed the hand up the arm to see who was attached to the other end. Sally Hayes, the high school principal. Salt and pepper hair and a designer suit. No mistake. Bella lifted her brows. "What are you doing here, Sally?"

"I was driving by and saw the crowd. I agree with them both, Mirabella." she said, nodding toward Jonathon Hawthorne and his daughter. "Go get yourself checked out. I insist. I'll handle your classes myself today if we can't get a sub."

There was an odd look on her face, though. A speculative look, and as Bella took her case from the woman she thought she realized why. A paper bag was clearly visible, sticking up from a side pouch on the case. The logo on the bag was a Witch on a broomstick in black silhouette, and the words *Gwenyth's Chamber* were stamped across the top.

She'd picked up a few supplies while visiting Gwen this morning. But she'd put the bag in the center portion of the briefcase, and she thought she'd zipped it. Apparently, though she hadn't. Somehow, it must have fallen free during the near miss, and Sally Hayes had tucked it back into the briefcase.

Which could mean she knew what was in it.

Nothing all that incriminating, really. A handful of altar candles in various colors, some patchouli oil, and a plastic zipper bag full of Gwen's homegrown rue. It shouldn't make Bella feel suddenly nervous or worried. But it did.

"Now you see?" the man was asking. "Everyone agrees you should be looked at. And besides, you just saved my daughter's life. It's the least I can do."

Reluctantly, knowing full well she shouldn't, Mirabella nodded. "All right." Frankly, she just wanted to be out of the spotlight as soon as possible. She didn't like all these people milling around looking at her. It was too much like the dream.

"Good." Jonathon Hawthorne turned to his daughter. "Maybe you'd better be checked out too. What do you think?"

"I didn't even get a scraped knee, Dad," Rowan said. "Miss Saint A landed on the pavement, and I landed on top of her. I'm fine. But I'll go see the school nurse before first period if you want."

"You do that," he sent the principal a glance.

"I'll make sure she does," Sally Hayes said. Then she smiled at Mirabella. "You're a hero today, Mirabella. Take the whole day off, if you like. And let me know if you need more time."

"Thank you," Bella said.

"Come along, Rowan. You can walk the rest of the way to school with me."

Rowan averted her face from the principal's view before she rolled her eyes. "Dad's going to drop me off, Mrs. Hayes. It's on the way to the clinic."

"Oh. All right then," Sally said.

Rowan's father turned Bella around, one hand on her arm, as if he thought she might fall again at any moment, and led her and his daughter across the street. His shiny black car stood cockeyed where he'd apparently skidded to a halt in panic at seeing his daughter nearly flattened by a truck. He opened the front passenger door, took Bella's briefcase from her, and held it as she got in. Then he leaned in, fastened her seatbelt for her, and handed the case back to her.

Bella shoved the *Gwenyth's Chamber* bag deeper into the front pouch, out of sight.

Rowan got into the back seat, and a second later, her father was behind the wheel and pulling away.

CHAPTER 3

He drove, she rode, and neither of them spoke much once they'd dropped Rowan at school. But he kept finding his gaze drawn to her, and since she mostly stared out the window, it was easy enough to look his fill. He wasn't sure what there was about the woman that should send warm waves of pleasure surging through his insides every time he touched her or looked too deeply into her eyes. Probably no more than the fact that he'd just seen her save his daughter's life, and his daughter was everything to him.

Yeah. That was all it was.

Her hair wasn't all that striking-even though it was the blue black of a raven's wing. And her eyes were *not* that enticing-just because their marbled green color was so vivid. Like malachite. Probably colored contacts, he imagined. And her shape was nothing to get this worked up about. Sure, she was willowy, leggy, lithe. But so were a lot of women these days. It wasn't that unusual.

The only thing different about her was her heroism in the face of a speeding truck. And the dirty smudges on her proper pearl-colored skirt and matching blazer. The run in her nylons. The bruise on her pretty cheek where she'd come between his precious Rowan and the pavement

Yeah. No wonder she looked good to him. It wasn't attraction. It couldn't be attraction, because he didn't *do* attraction. Hadn't been drawn to another woman since Ashley died.

"I...um....can get someone to bring my car to the clinic. You can just drop me and go on your way. I don't want to make you late for work," she said, when she turned and caught him staring.

"I think the DA's office will survive the morning without me."

She went a little stiller, and he saw her eyes flare just slightly wider. "You're a prosecutor?"

"Not nearly as exciting as it sounds. Ezra Township is pretty much typical of the entire district. Rural. Quiet. We don't see a lot of crime out here. At least...not until recently."

He parked the car, got out, and she did too, even before he could get around it to open her door. He walked close to her, in case she had another dizzy spell or stumbled. Or...that was why he told himself he was walking so close. She shivered when his arm brushed hers, and he wondered why. Was she feeling this odd attraction as well?

"Are you talking about the animal mutilations, Mr. Hawthorne?"

"Disgusting, isn't it?" He sighed and shook his head.

They stopped outside the door of the clinic, and she turned, looked up at him. "Do you think the police have any idea who's behind them?"

"I'm sure they do. But um...I can't really discuss it beyond that."

"Of course not."

He opened the door, held it for her, and she went inside. He stood back while she checked in at the receptionist's desk.

Then she came back to him. "It's a slow day," she said. "They can get me right in."

"Great. I'll be waiting."

She bit her lower lip, worrying it with her teeth in a way that made his stomach clench up. He said, "Unless...you're not comfortable with me sticking around a bit longer. I only want to be sure you're all right."

"No. I....No. It's fine."

She *was* uncomfortable with him. He could tell. It made him wonder why. Made him want to find out. He supposed that was in his nature. His role at work lent itself to a good deal of investigating. Legwork. Some of the lawyers in the office preferred to hire investigators. He preferred to do it himself.

He sat down, picked up a magazine, and watched her disappear through the door and into the exam room. A half-hour later, she came out again, and the only real difference he saw was that she'd washed the smudges off her face. Dr. Plummer came out behind her, a chart in her hand. She was the stereotype of a small town doctor in every way except gender. She was aging, white haired, kindly, and brilliant.

Jonathon got to his feet. "Well?"

"I'll live," Mirabella said with a nervous little smile.

The doctor looked up from the chart. "She probably has a slight concussion, but that's not serious."

"Then...she should be in a hospital, shouldn't she?" Mirabella sent him a quick frown, but he pretended not to notice.

"Not necessarily," Dr. Plummer said. "She just needs watching for the next twenty-four hours. Any vomiting, fainting, severe dizziness, just call me. I don't think there will be."

He licked his lips, sent Mirabella a silent look. She sent one right back, telling him to keep his mouth shut. He did, but he didn't like it. She hitched her purse up higher on her shoulder, thanked the doctor with a smile, and headed out of the clinic. Jonathon really had no choice but to follow.

He waited until they were back in the car, no longer. "So how are you going to be watched closely for twenty-four hours if you live alone?"

She swung her dark eyes right up to meet his. "How do you know I live alone?"

"Well, I...I mean, I assumed...." He frowned. Since when did he stammer around a female? "It is *Miss* Saint Angeline, isn't it?"

She shrugged. "Sure. But I could live with someone."

"Do you?"

She averted her eyes. "No, but that's beside the point."

"Actually, it's not." He sighed. "So where do you live? I'll drive you home."

"I'm not going home. I'm going to school."

He braced his hands on the wheel, turned to look her dead in the eye, and said, "Please don't."

She blinked as if in surprise.

"Look. I'm way out of practice at this knight in shining armor routine. And if I take you to work, and you keel over halfway through the day, it's gonna ruin the entire effort. *And* make me look really bad to my daughter."

Her expression softened a little. He thought she might have almost smiled. "She means a lot to you, your daughter."

"Rowan is all I have in the world."

She frowned, tilted her head to one side. "I think your wife would disagree with that."

"My wife died ten years ago."

"I'm so sorry," she said. "I...didn't realize...."

"Look, the point is, you are my daughter's favorite teacher. And I had every intention of calling you today anyway. And now you've gone and hurt yourself protecting

Rowan from a runaway truck, and you don't even want to let me see you home. Put yourself in my shoes for a minute, will you?"

She looked at him oddly, as if she suspected him of some dire ulterior motive. But softly, she said, "All right. You can take me home. It's out on Sycamore."

"That's only a few blocks from us. We're on Highland." He smiled and put the car in gear, pulled out of the parking lot and headed toward her house.

"And on the way," she said, "maybe you can tell me why you were planning to call me today."

"Right." He took a breath, chose his words with care. The last thing he wanted was to say anything that seemed negative about his daughter. She was brilliant, and deep, and thoughtful and wonderful. "I wanted to talk about Rowan." He glanced sideways at her, watching her reactions.

A quick frown bent her brows and she looked at him intently, all defenses, all wariness gone. He liked that, that swift, concerned reaction. "Why"? Is something wrong?"

"I was hoping you could tell me."

HE DROPPED her off at her home, insisted on walking her to the door, and left his card with his beeper and cell phone numbers on the back for her to use in case she needed anything.

She went inside, closed the door, and watched him until his car was out of sight. Then she snatched up the phone and called Gwenyth.

"I know who he is!" she all but shouted when her best friend picked up.

"What? Who? Bella, what are you talking about?"

"The man. In the dream! I know who he is. His name is

Jonathon Hawthorne and he's a prosecutor for the district attorney's office. His daughter is a student of mine. Rowan."

She could almost see Gwen's frown. "Is this the girl you pushed out of the path of that truck this morning?"

"Yes!"

"And that was her father you drove away with?"

"Yes!"

"Are you freaking out of your mind, Mirabella?"

"Yes! No. I don't know." Bella pushed a hand through her hair and paced the room. "He said he was going to call me anyway today. To talk to me about Rowan. He says she's been going through some drastic changes, lately, and he's worried about her."

"What is she? Thirteen? Fourteen?"

"Fourteen."

"And he's worried about changes?" Gwen blew a sigh. "Fourteen-year-olds are made up of changes. If you cut them open, changes are what you see writhing around in their insides. What is he, from Mars or something?"

Bella paced the floor, licking her lips. "No, there's more to it. He was holding a lot back, I could tell. But he was talking to me about her...he says she's starting to show interest in the Craft-or, the 'occult' as he calls it. She's been asking questions that make him uncomfortable. And he seems determined to put a stop to it."

"Do you blame him? The only things he probably knows-thinks he knows-about the Craft are butchered kitties and defaced tombstones." She sighed. "Why doesn't he have Rowan's mother talk to her? I mean, women tend to understand these things...."

"She's dead. Died ten years ago, he said."

"Oh. Oh."

"I don't know what to do here. Gwen. I mean...if I talk to Rowan about the Craft-"

"You can't do that! Good grief, after that dream? Are you insane?"

"But in the dream the girl committed suicide! If she knew the truth about things, that never would have happened. Maybe it was because I didn't get to her soon enough. Maybe she's going to get involved with this group of phony wannabes who go around murdering animals. Maybe my telling her would-"

"He's a prosecutor. You saw a vision that was supposed to warn you away from this pair, not send you straight to the stake!"

"That part was symbolic and you know it."

Gwen sniffed indignantly. '"You hope."

Mirabella sighed. "I'm going to go meditate on this for awhile. I'll call you later, okay?"

"Sure. Later. In the meantime, though, hon. be careful. Watch your back. I mean it."

"I will." With a sigh, she hung up the phone.

Several hours later, Bella's doorbell chimed.

Mirabella turned toward it, only to see Rowan Hawthorne standing on the other side, looking in at her.

CHAPTER 4

Jonathon sat in on the unofficial questioning of Bryan Marcomb. Bryan was seventeen, all limbs, with dark greasy hair and a goatee he must have thought looked cool. His mother had brought him in at the police department's request. He had a lawyer with him, but not a very good one. The guy was dead silent throughout the interview.

"You understand, you're not being charged with anything yet," Officer Cantone said. "But you *were* seen running away from that cemetery the other night. We know you were there." The final line was delivered with a grimness that let the kid know he was in trouble. Cantone was a good guy-his only faults, so far as Jonathon could tell, were a beer belly and a lack of tolerance for the foolishness of youth.

The kid rolled his eyes.

Cantone narrowed his. "The only reason we haven't charged you yet is because we haven't decided what to charge you *with*? The kid's eyes widened just a little. "What, you're surprised by that?" the officer asked him. "You thought we brought you down here to play patty-cake? All I wanna know is this—did you participate in whatever sick little party was going on out there that night? Or were you just a spectator?"

The kid lowered his gaze and pressed his lips together.

His harried looking, dough-faced mother gripped his arm and squeezed. "Answer the policeman, Bryan."

With a sigh. Bryan looked up at Cantone again. "I was just hanging out."

"Then why did you run?" the cop asked.

He shrugged. "Why'd you chase me? When someone chases me, I tend to run."

Cantone's sigh should have sent papers flying off desks. "Look, you couldn't have been there and not seen something. So either you tell me what it is, or I have to assume you're a part of it! Got that?"

No reaction. The cop looked at the mother. "I thought you said he'd cooperate."

"She don't speak for me," Bryan spat. "I don't know anything. I'm not saying anything."

For just a second there was something in the kid's eyes. Something that made Jonathon frown and look closer. It had been brief, that flash. But for just a second, the kid had looked afraid. Truly afraid.

Almost as afraid as Mirabella Saint Angeline had looked when she'd first seen him this morning, Jonathon thought. And then he wondered how she was doing and thought about giving her a call. The woman had been haunting his thoughts all day. He could get lost in her eyes, even when he only saw them in his mind. What the hell was it about her?

He forced his mind back to the task at hand, back to the kid.

"Have you ever been inside a shop called *Gwenyth's Chamber*, Bryan?" Officer Cantone asked.

"That Witch shop in town, you mean? Sure, I've been in

there. She has cool stuff. What's that got to do with anything?"

"Just let me ask the questions, here, all right? What kind of cool stuff does she have that interests you?"

"I don't know, just stuff."

"Do you know the owner?"

Bryan frowned. "The blonde who runs the place? Not really." Bryan looked at his mother. "Can we just go now? Please?"

Mrs. Marcomb pursed her lips, looking mad as hell. But Jonathon thought it was more worry for her son than real anger. She loved the kid, though he was probably driving her nuts.

"You can go," Jonathon said. When Officer Cantone opened his mouth to object, Jonathon shot him a silent message. The cop read it, and nodded, and the mother and son hurried out of there.

"He was there," Cantone said.

"Yeah, but he's not fooling anyone with that tough-boy routine. I don't know if he's a part of this or not, but I do know he thinks he's in serious trouble if he talks to us. He was scared, Billy."

"So what do you suggest we do?" Cantone asked.

"I think you gave him a lot to think about here. Let's give him a few days. I have a feeling he'll be back."

Pursing his lips, the cop nodded. "Okay, we'll try it your way."

Jonathon left and hurried down the hall to his own office in the small, two-story County Building in Branwich, the biggest town in the district, which was still a small town by most standards. It boasted a Wal-Mart, a handful of grocery and drug stores, one movie theater and two pizza places. Ezra Township was fourteen miles away.

He closed his office door, picked up the phone, and

punched in Mirabella Saint Angeline's number...which, for some reason, he'd already committed to memory. Probably from having almost dialed it at least ten times today. He supposed it was natural to want to check in, make sure she was all right. Hell, she was all alone out there in her little cobblestone cottage with its vine covered walls and its big front porch. He didn't think he'd ever seen so many sets of wind chimes in one place before.

Her telephone rang three times. He was about to hang up and head over there to check in person, when she picked up on the fourth ring.

"HELLO?"

"Mirabella?"

Bella heard him say her name, and she shivered down deep in reaction to it. It wasn't just out of fear, either. There was something deeper. Something primal that experienced the sound of his voice like a physical touch.

It occurred to her that it was the first time he'd called her by her first name. And for some insane reason, she responded the same way. "Jonathon," she said, when she could catch her breath. "I'm...surprised to hear from you."

It was a lie. She'd been all but staring at the phone waiting for his call today. She lifted her gaze as she spoke, to watch his daughter, pacing in the next room. Mirabella had only just let her in when the telephone had interrupted them.

"I thought I'd check in. Just to, you know, make sure everything's still okay."

"Everything's fine."

"No dizzy spells or anything?"

"Not a one."

"Good."

He went silent for a long moment. She cleared her throat. "I...have company." she said. "So I really should—"

"Man or woman?" he asked.

She blinked in surprise at the bluntness of that question. But licking her lips she said. "Woman. Why?"

"Curiosity got the best of me, I guess. I, um... never mind."

"No. Tell me, what were you going to say?"

When he spoke again, his voice was much deeper, and a lot softer. "I haven't been able to stop thinking about you all day." He paused. "I know, that sounds like the world's worst pick up line. It wasn't."

"I know."

"Do you?" He cleared his throat uneasily. "Does that mean you feel there might be...something going on here. Between us?"

She closed her eyes, and her stomach knotted up. "There's something, Jonathon."

He sighed as if in relief. "I'm glad it's not just me. If you knew how unlike me this is. I...." He stopped there. "You said you had company. I'll let you go."

"Thanks."

"But I'll call again later on."

She shook her head. "You don't need to."

"Actually, I think I do."

She frowned "What's that supposed to mean?"

"Damned if I know. I'll talk to you later, okay?"

"Okay."

"Take it easy. Rest, like the doc said."

"I will. Good-bye, Jonathon."

"Bye."

She hung up the phone, stared at it for a moment, and wondered why her heart was fluttering wildly in her chest. Why the stroke of each tone of his voice against her eardrums had been an erotic experience. Why she was breathless by the time she said good-bye.

She gathered her composure, bit by bit, and finally, lifted her chin, and walked back into the parlor where Rowan waited. "Sorry for the interruption. We can talk now. Please, sit down."

Rowan did, choosing the claw legged chair with the embroidered upholstery and looking like a nervous princess, taking her throne. The girl was nothing less than stunning. And her eyes could stop traffic.

"How's my dad?" she asked.

Mirabella blinked. "You were listening?"

"Only a little. Thanks for not telling him I was here."

"I didn't think he'd approve of you leaving school over an hour early any more than I do. Care to tell me why you did that?"

She shrugged. "I told Principal Hayes I was shaken up and sore from the accident. But really I just wanted to come and see you."

"To make sure I was okay?" Mirabella asked.

Rowan lowered her eyes. "Partly that."

"Well, I'm okay. So we can go on to the other part."

The girl licked her lips, lifted her head slowly, and stabbed Bella's eyes with her own. "Are you a Witch?"

Mirabella lifted her eyebrows and sucked in a breath. It took her a moment to formulate a reply, but she managed to find one. "That's a very personal question, Rowan. Maybe a little bit too personal. May I ask what makes you want to know?"

"Because...you can do things. And I want to know what it means."

Bella waited, but Rowan stopped there. "Well, come on, Rowan. Don't leave me hanging. What kinds of things are you talking about?"

Biting her lower lip, Rowan got to her feet, paced to the middle of the room, and turned to face Mirabella. "You shouted that warning before the truck ever came into sight. You knew it was coming."

Lowering her head, Bella closed her eyes at the pealing of the warning bells in her mind. "How do you know I didn't just hear the truck coming?"

"Because I didn't hear it."

"You had your headphones on."

"I yanked them off. There was no sound-not until a second or two later."

Bella shook her head slowly and got to her feet. She didn't mention the woman she'd seen pointing frantically, because when she'd looked around for her in the moments after the near miss-she hadn't seen her. And she knew damn well that was because the woman wasn't someone physical. She was a spirit.

Bella said none of this to Rowan. Instead, she said. "Come with me. We need tea."

Rowan followed her into the kitchen, where Bella put on a kettle of water, and dug two antique metal tea balls from a drawer. She opened her cupboard, on rows of glass jars, each containing herbs most of which either she or Gwyneth had grown, dried, and ground themselves. As she dipped from one of the jars, she said, "This is my special, calming blend. Chamomile, valerian, a bit of lavender." She measured tea into each tea ball, then dropped them into a pair of china cups, leaving their chains dangling over the sides. Rowan took a seat at the small round table.

"So you think I sensed that truck coming before I could see or hear it?" Mirabella asked.

"Yes. I know you did."

"And that makes you think I might be a Witch?"

Rowan shook her head. "More than just that. I saw you

coming out of that shop. *Gwenyth 's Chamber.* And you bought stuff in there. It was in your briefcase."

"I like herbs. I make homemade teas. Does that make me a Witch then?" She was stalling, really. Fishing. She knew too well that Rowan was the girl in her dream. And she was scared to death of the idea that the child could die because of something Bella might teach her. Apparently, something about Witchcraft. She had to be extremely careful what she said to this child.

She heard the water start to boil and poured it into the cups. Then she carried them to the table, went to the fridge for cream, set out the sugar, and finally sat down and moved the tea ball by its chain in slow circles in the cup, to calm her nerves.

"Rowan, why don't we chalk it up to women's intuition and call it good, hmm?" She sipped again. "After all, why should it matter what I am?" She took a sip of her tea, but it was still weak.

"Because I need to know what I am. Am I a Witch, Miss Saint A? Is there any way to tell?"

The tea sort of gushed backward up Bella's windpipe and out her nose.

Now that she'd started, though. Rowan rushed right on, speaking faster with every sentence and barely pausing for a breath in between. "The other day, someone called me a name in the hall at school, and I turned around, really angry, and when I did, the posters fell off the walls. All the way up the hall from where I was standing to where the other person was. It was a good ten feet. And I knew it was that rush of anger that knocked them all down. It was like I could feel it surging out of me, you know. And then last night, my dad got on my case for some stupid thing or other, and I went up to my room, spun around to slam the door, only it slammed itself, before I ever touched it." She set her tea down, got to her feet, and paced the room. "Miss Saint A, stuff like that happens to me all the time. More than just what could be coincidence or explained away. More than I can understand. Dad says it's all in my head, and to tell you the truth I was beginning to wonder if he was right. But then my mother started coming to me...in my dreams. And it's like she's trying to tell me something, and I don't know what it is, and-"

Tears seemed to choke her. They welled up in her eyes, and her voice got tighter until it tightened into silence.

Bella got up and went to her, clasped her shoulders, and looked right into her ocean blue eyes. "You're *not* crazy. There's nothing wrong or even all that unusual about what's happening to you, Rowan."

Rowan sniffled and brushed at her eyes. "Really?"

"I promise. I...." Mirabella closed her eyes, bit her lip. Hell, she was risking her job and Jonathon's anger by even saying a little. But the girl was in pain. What choice did she have? Could she really just bite her tongue and watch this incredible young woman suffer?

No. She couldn't.

So she chose her words carefully. "I believe we all have more than the five senses we acknowledge. A lot of other people believe it too. Doctors, scientists, world leaders."

Blinking, searching her eyes. Rowan said, "What kinds of senses?"

Bella shrugged. "Oh, psychism or telekinesis. Picking up on thoughts. Causing physical movement by the power of will and emotion. And there are lots of other extra senses we have too. Precognition...."

"Like when I reach for the phone before it rings, and already know who's on the other end. Or hum a song and turn on the radio and hear it playing?"

"Yes. Just like that. It's pretty widely accepted by those who study such things, that there are two times in life when these...other senses...are naturally strongest. One is when we're very young. Babies, toddlers. Before society has convinced us that such things don't exist. And the other time, is during puberty. Particularly in girls."

The relief that flooded Rowan's face made Mirabella know it was worth the risk. She'd said very little. And somehow, she had given Rowan something she'd desperately needed; validation, assurance that she wasn't losing her mind.

"You're not just saying this to make me feel better?"

"No. I'm not."

She smiled, though her tears were spilling over now. Down her cheeks. "Then...everyone has these powers? Not just...Witches?"

"Everyone has them to one degree or another. Witchcraft is just the name given to the art of mastering them, learning to control them, and make them stronger. Well-that's a part of it, anyway."

"And what's the rest of it?"

Mirabella lowered her eyes. "You haven't even tasted your tea.'"

Rowan returned to her seat, calmer now, and sipped the tea, then licked her lips and sipped it again. "It's good," she said. "Miss Saint A, what do you think my mom is trying to tell me?"

"I don't know. Maybe she's just letting you know she's still with you, watching over you," Mirabella mused, returning to her seat as well.

Rowan seemed to think on that for a moment. "I don't think that's it. She always seems...agitated. Worried about something. Her lips move like she's trying to say something, but I just can't hear her."

Frowning. Mirabella sensed the girl was not referring to a dream. Not an ordinary one, anyway.

Funny, how they'd both received messages during dream-time, neither of which could be cast off as dreams. And how they seemed to be on a path that was determined to cross. "What was your mother's name. Rowan?"

"Ashley." she said, softly, wistfully. "Ashley Rowan Hawthorne. And I'm Rowan Ashley."

There was a powerful mother-child bond at work here. She could feel it clearly. "How do you feel when she comes to you?" she asked, hoping to get some clue what the message might be.

Rowan closed her eyes. "First...it's just joy to see her. She's so beautiful. And so real. Dad says I look just like her. But I think he's exaggerating. Sometimes I wish I didn't have to wake up at all, just so I could still be with her."

A little bolt of alarm shot through Bella. "She wouldn't want that. Rowan—for you to leave this lifetime before you were meant to. She wouldn't want that at all."

Rowan studied her, tilting her head to one side. "I know that." Then, sighing deeply, she took a small pouch out of her pocket. "I found this in the trunk in the attic, where my dad keeps all my mom's things." Gently, she opened the pouch, and tipped it up so its contents spilled out onto the table. A handful of crystals-quartz, tiger's eye, amber, and jet. Some rose petals. A seashell. A bit of hair, its color so deeply auburn it had to have been Rowan's own. The lock was fine, curling, baby hair, bound in a pink ribbon. There was a feather, raven or perhaps crow. And a silver five-pointed star, enclosed with a circle, on a long chain.

"Does your father know you have this?"

'"No. He wouldn't like it. Does it mean what I think it means? Was my mother...was she a Witch?" Rowan picked up the pentacle. "Isn't this an evil symbol?"

Bella closed her hand over Rowan's around the star, then turning it palm up, opened the girl's fingers. She traced the star with her own. "Earth." she said, tracing the point in the three o'clock position. "That's your body and your home." She traced another point "Air, your mind and your breath." Tracing the next, she said, "Water, your blood and your emotions." And the next. "Fire, your energy and your passion." Finally, she moved her finger over the topmost point "Spirit—the life force that lives in all of us.

"What most people call God or Goddess, is, to me, the Source from which we come, to which we return, and of which we are always a part. It's alive in each of us, and it's the sum total of us all. That's what the circle around the star means. That we're all connected. That's what your mother believed in, Rowan. That's why she wore this symbol There's nothing evil about that."

Another tear, a relieved one. Bella thought, rolled slowly down Rowan's ivory cheek. She smiled, sniffed noisily. "Then she wasn't into murdering cats or anything like that?"

Bella was probably getting herself in too deep. But she had come this far. She didn't suppose she could make things much worse by giving the girl one more kernel of knowledge, to ease her mind. "There's one cardinal rule in the Craft of the Wise, Rowan. And that is to harm none. No true Witch would hurt another living thing."

Rowan looked up, eyes widening slowly. "You know so much about this...does that mean, you really are...?"

"Yeah. I really am. But if it gets out, Rowan, especially with the stuff that's been going on in town lately, I could be in a lot of trouble. Not everyone understands. Not everyone wants to."

"I'm not going to say anything to anyone," Rowan promised.

"I don't want you to lie either. If you're asked, tell the truth. The thing is...by talking to you at all, I'm putting us both in an awkward position. I don't feel very good about discussing this stuff with you behind your father's back."

Rowan lowered her head. "I don't understand why he's so against it. I mean, he had to know about Mom."

"Maybe you need to talk to him. Openly and honestly. If you can get his permission, I'll help you learn to understand more about it all."

"But what if he says no?"

Mirabella lowered her eyes. "Then I'll give you suggestions for some good books on the subject and...and then, I don't know. We'll see." Reaching out, she stroked the girl's hair. "I promise you, it's better to be honest with him from the start. You don't want to get into the habit of sneaking around, hiding things, and lying to him. It can only lead to trouble."

She sighed heavily. Bella knew she disagreed. "Listen, whatever you do, no drastic measures, okay? I'm on your side. Please remember that. And when it comes down to it, so is your dad. No one loves you more than he does."

"I know that."

"So?"

She drew a breath, nodded as she blew it out again. "Okay. At least I know I'm not crazy."

"No. You just inherited a special gift from your mom. More than one, even." She nodded at the little empty pouch on the table. "That was your mother's power bag. Put the things back inside and keep it with you all the lime. A lot of her energy lingers in those things. I felt it when I touched the pent. When you want to feel her near you, take them out, hold them. Wear the necklace if you want, under your blouse for now. But don't let anyone else handle them. You can add your own special treasures when they turn up, if you want to. Maybe hand it down to your own daughter one day."

Rowan looked at her for a second, then she reached

across the table, slid her hand over Bella's, and squeezed it just once. "You don't know how much this talk means to me," she whispered. "Thank you, Miss Saint A."

"I think you may as well call me Bella, outside school, all right?" she said. Inexplicably, she felt tears brimming in her own eyes. "Now, do you need a ride home?"

"I've got the four-wheeler."

"And a helmet. I hope?"

Rowan rolled her eyes. "You sound like my father."

Bella walked her through the house, to the front door, and watched her leave. Then she turned to head back to the kitchen to clean up the tea cups, but when she passed by the antique oval mirror in the hallway, she stopped in her tracks, jerked her head to the side, and stared wide eyed at her own reflection.

A pale skinned, auburn haired woman stood just behind her, but only for an instant. She met Bella's eyes with an intense, unreadable expression, then faded almost at once.

Dad says I look just like her....

Ashley, she thought. That's who the ghost was. She had to be Ashley Hawthorne. Rowan's mother.

Jonathon's wife.

CHAPTER 5

By five-thirty. Jonathan had resisted calling her a half dozen more times. But the temptation remained, even while he drove the car home. So he postponed the inevitable by calling Rowan first.

She snapped up the phone on ring number two, and her "hello" was so cheerful that he held the phone away from his ear and blinked at it in shock. Then he drew it back again. "Rowan?" he asked.

"Hi. Dad. Are you on your way home?"

"Yeah, I am. You sound in a good mood. Should I take that to mean you're fully recovered from your brush with disaster this morning?"

"Fully," she said. "I'm as good as new. I was a little shaky, but then I talked to Miss Saint A this afternoon, and she-"

"She went to school today?" he asked.

"No. Actually...." She sighed.

"Actually?" he prompted.

"Miss Saint A says I shouldn't get into the habit of keeping things from you, so here goes nothing. I went home early. And I decided to go by her house to see how she was doing."

He was quiet for a moment. "Thank you for that," he said softly.

"You're not mad?"

"No. Are you okay, hon? I thought you said you were feeling better."

"Oh, I am. Now."

"Good. So how was she, when you saw her?"

"She was great, Dad. I mean, she wound up giving me some herbal tea and making me feel better. Even though she's the one who got banged up this morning."

He nodded slowly. "So it's safe to say she wasn't resting when you got there."

"No. Not really. Dad...I was there when you called."

"Oh?" He tugged his tie loose and undid the top button of his shirt.

"I know you like her."

He licked his lips, shook his head at the phone. "I only just met her, Rowan."

"I know. She's like that. I mean, I liked her the first time I met her too, and I usually hate teachers on sight, even if I don't know them yet. There's something...special about Bella, though."

He lowered his head, gnawed his lip. His daughter was too perceptive for his own peace of mind.

"And I hate to think of her all alone in that big house making her own dinner tonight. I mean, after what she did this morning-"

"You want to invite her to dinner?" He battled a smile.

"Can we?"

"I guess. I don't know if she'll come, but-"

"Why don't you stop and ask her? It's on your way home anyway."

Yes, it was on his way home. He'd already been looking

forward to driving by and trying to catch a glimpse of her as he passed. What was it about the woman...?

"Dad?"

"What? Oh, yeah. It's on the way. I'll stop and deliver the invitation. Good idea, Rowan."

"I know it was," she said. "So I'll see you later, then?"

"Sure will. Love you, kiddo."

"You too, Dad."

"Rowan?"

"Hmm?"

He swallowed hard. "Thanks for being up front with me. You always can, you know. No matter what."

"It works both ways, Dad," she said.

He paused, sighed. "You're right. There is something...special about Bella."

"I know."

The phone clicked, and he folded his in half and tucked it back into his pocket. Then he turned onto Sycamore, two blocks up, and into Mirabella Saint Angeline's gravel driveway. His feet crunched over the stones, tapped up the steps and across the porch, and then he rang the doorbell. He waited a few beats. No one answered. He tried listening for footsteps from within, but the place was far too noisy for that. She had at least a dozen sets of wind chimes out there, and beyond the tinkling of them, there were the birds. She had more birds flitting around than any other house on the block. Frowning, he rang the bell again, then peered through the glass. Odd.

He was just about to start imagining she'd had complications from that bump on the head and was lying unconscious somewhere inside, when he heard a sound from beyond the house-one loud enough to be heard above the din. The back yard? He trotted down off the porch and around back. And there she was, standing on a wobbly ladder, pouring birdseed into a feeder. Which, he supposed accounted for all the birds.

"Now that's what I call taking it easy," he remarked.

She jerked her head around, apparently startled. The ladder tipped. The bag of seed hit the ground with a thump, and Jonathon shot forward to prevent the lady from doing the same. The next thing he knew she was in his arms. She'd fallen, and he'd caught her, awkwardly. His arms were tight around her thighs, and his face was pressed to her abdomen...mostly. Her hands braced on his shoulders. A rush of desire rose up inside him like a sleeping dragon that had been poked with a sharp stick. It had been a long time since he'd been this close to a woman or held a feminine body this tightly to his. And in spite of his usually chivalrous nature, he took advantage. He lowered her slowly. His face slid over her belly, pushing her shirt up a little on the way. His five o'clock shadow rasped over her skin. He heard her catch her breath. To his credit he pulled back a little to let her breasts slide by his face without *quite* touching, but he held tightly enough so the rest of her was pressed to the rest of him all the way down, until her feet touched the ground.

His arms locked around her waist, her body flush against his and warm and soft, her face, only a breath away, there was just no stopping it. He kissed her. He didn't think about it first, and he didn't ask permission. He just bent his head and covered her mouth with his. Her lips parted on a soft sigh, and her arms curled around his neck. She kissed him back. Her tongue met his, stroked it, teased and tangled with it, and he trembled all over with heat and hunger and need.

God, it had been so long....

He kissed her for a long, long time. He picked her up off her feet again, and she wrapped her legs around him, hooked her ankles at his back. He cupped her head in one hand and her bottom in the other, and he fed from her lips like a man starving to death. And finally, he lifted his head just a little, and breathlessly, he said. "I don't know what this is...."

"I don't either," she whispered.

"God, I want you. It doesn't make sense. It's too fast, too damn sudden, but...."

"I know. I know, Jonathon. It's the same for me."

He kissed her again. Felt his own arousal pressed tight between her legs and cursed the clothes they were wearing as he moved against her there.

She broke the kiss this time. Panting, breathless, her eyes heavy and passion-glazed, she whispered, "There are things you don't know about me, Jonathon. Things I have to tell you, before-"

The bleating sound of his telephone ringing cut her off. He stared into her eyes for a moment longer, while it rang again. He was out of breath, and his heart was thundering against her.

She untwined from him, put her feet on the ground, averted her eyes, and said, "You'd better get it."

Nodding, never taking his eyes off her, he pulled the cell phone from his pocket, flipped it open, and brought it to his ear.

"Daddy?"

It was Rowan. And the ragged sound of her voice jerked him roughly back into his right mind again. He blinked away the haze of passion or whatever the hell had been fogging his brain. "Rowan? Honey, what is it? What's wrong?"

Mirabella's face changed too, as she searched his with worry in her eyes.

"Oh. Dad, it's awful. I mean, I'm fine, but Shauna...."

"Shauna Gordon?" he asked.

"It's awful, Dad. Just come home. Come home right now. Please?"

"I'm on my way." He wasn't even fully aware of gripping

Mirabella's hand and pulling her along beside him until they were both in the car. He didn't think it had ever once occurred to her not to come along.

"What is it?" Bella asked. "Is she okay?"

"I think so. She said it wasn't her. It's something about her best friend."

"Yes, Shauna, I heard that much. She didn't say what?"

"No. Thank God we're so close."

MIRABELLA HAD BEEN LOST in his kiss, his touch, his very presence. But Rowan's phone call snapped her out of that in a hurry, and it was only moments before Jonathon was skidding to a stop in his own driveway.

It wasn't far from where her own house was, physically. Socially it was a world away. On his street, people lived in huge houses with paved driveways and swimming pools. The Hawthorne house was set apart from the others, around a curve in the narrow lane, and up a slight hill. It was bigger, fancier. Big brick fireplace chimney creeping up one side and floor to ceiling windows angling up all the way into the peak at the front. Cedar and glass. Welcoming rather than pretentious.

Jonathon cut the engine, and Mirabella drew a deep breath before getting out, wondering what was coming next. There was a distinct feeling of taking her life into her hands happening here. Not by rushing to Rowan's rescue at Jonathon's side. She couldn't help doing that. She wouldn't be who she was if she did any differently.

It was the dream. The warning. Someone was trying hard to warn her and Rowan. Mirabella wished to the heavens she knew why.

Jonathon opened the front door and clasped her hand again as he hurried into the house, through a foyer and living room that would have impressed anyone, into the smaller dining room beyond. That was where he stopped and just stood in the doorway, looking at his daughter.

Rowan was sitting on the floor, legs curled in front of her, phone to her ear, tear tracks streaking her pretty face. She looked up, met her father's eyes, and said, "My dad's here, Shauna. I'll call you back, okay? Will you be all right? Okay. No, really, only a few minutes. Promise. Bye." Rowan's lower lip trembled as she got to her feet. She dropped the cordless phone onto the table and met her father halfway across the room.

Jonathon folded her into his arms. "It's okay, baby. Whatever it is, it's all right. What happened to Shauna? Hmm?"

She shook her head against his chest. "Not Shauna, her boyfriend. He...God, I don't know if I can even say it. He hanged himself."

"Oh my God." Jonathon clutched her closer, his hand in her hair. "Honey, I'm so sorry. Was...was he a friend of yours, too?"

She gently extricated herself from her father's arms. "I knew him. We weren't close or anything, but...poor Shauna. She's so crushed over this. And I don't know what to say to her or how to make it better." She turned her gaze to Mirabella's then, sniffing and swiping at her eyes. "I'm so glad you're here."

"Of course I am, Rowan. As long as you need me." She opened her arms, and Rowan came and hugged her, too.

"Why would he do it, Bella?" Rowan asked. "Why would Bryan do something like this?"

Mirabella had been trying to put it together in her mind and hearing the boy's first name finally clicked it into place.

Bryan Marcomb. A junior in high school and a boy Mirabella knew as well as she knew any of the students. *God what a waste.* "Mrs. Marcomb must be devastated," she said, stroking Rowan's hair.

She saw Jonathon's frown, saw the look he sent her.

"I should call her back. I'm so worried about her being alone right now. Not that she's *really* alone. I mean, her parents are there, and her sisters, but..." She turned to her father. "Maybe I should go spend the night with her, just to-"

"No." He said it so quickly Mirabella knew something was up. But he softened his tone immediately. "I think your friend needs time to work through this, and I think she should probably spend it with her family. Just for a day or so. Then you can be there for her too. Right now it...it's just too fresh."

His cell phone was jangling again. He reached down, shut it off without answering it. "Go ahead, honey. Call Shauna back."

Rowan sniffed and nodded. She reached for the cordless phone, then hesitated. "I don't know what to say to her."

"You're doing just the right thing," Mirabella told her. "Just talking to her and listening. It doesn't matter what you say, because there really isn't anything that can help ease the pain. What counts is you being there for her. So you talk and you listen for as long as she needs you to. And you feel good about being the kind of friend who comes through at times like this. Okay?"

She nodded. "Thanks, Bella."

"You're welcome. And when you finish listening to her talk it out, you can turn right around and talk it out for yourself. To me, or your dad, or both of us if you need to, for as long as you need to, until you feel better. Okay?"

She smiled just a little. "It's so sad."

"Yes, it is. And totally senseless. Take note of that, Rowan.

Take note of the incredible amount of pain Bryan's act has caused you, and Shauna, and his mother, his friends. And I promise you, it hasn't solved whatever problems he thought he had. Life is meant to be lived. To the natural end." She spoke faster, gripping the girl's shoulders for emphasis. "When you take that way out, you're only going to have to start all over from square one the next time around. It solves nothing. It changes nothing. It's a lifetime that has to be repeated. Know that, Rowan. *Really* know it."

Looking at her oddly, Rowan nodded. "I do know it. Bella, is anything wrong?"

Bella lowered her eyes, releasing the girl's shoulders, and drawing a steadying breath. "No. Go ahead and call Shauna. She needs you right now."

Nodding. Rowan dialed her friend back again. As she reached her and began talking, Jonathon took Mirabella's arm and led her back into the living room.

"What was all that about? That reaction? Do you have some notion Rowan might be a suicide risk?"

She swallowed hard. "He was in her peer group, even if just by extension, Jonathon. I was just...taking precautions."

He tipped his head to one side. "You haven't seen any symptoms of-"

"No. Honestly. I haven't seen a hint of depression in Rowan."

He searched her eyes, then nodded, and sighed in relief. "This is awful. I just saw that kid this morning."

"What kid?"

"Bryan Marcomb." His face was grim as he turned to pace the room.

"Why?"

"He was seen running from the cemetery the night of the most recent animal mutilation."

Bella frowned. "Jonathon, do you think he was involved?"

"I don't know. But I think he knew who was. And I got the distinct feeling he was afraid to talk about it." He lowered his head. "Damn it, I'd hate to think he was so afraid he chose suicide over talking to the police." Then he sighed. "Probably not. It was probably some twisted occult thing that pushed him over the edge."

Jonathon assumed that the boy had been involved in the Craft. And that it was responsible for his death. She shivered, because this was so close to her dream...a child, committing suicide, an adult blaming it on Witchcraft. She had the distinct feeling they'd just moved yet another step closer to the final disaster.

She wanted with everything in her to tell Jonathon the truth. To set the record straight, come clean with him. But it just wasn't the right time. Already, he was turning his cell phone back on, hitting buttons. "That was my office before. No doubt calling to tell me about Marcomb's death." Then he paused in dialing, met her eyes, and offered a very slight smile. One hand rose to stroke her hair. "We have so much to talk about, you and I. I...I haven't felt this way in a very long time, Mirabella. I'm sorry all this had to come up now and get in the way."

"Rowan comes first," she told him. "And poor Bryan. You owe it to him to find out what's really going on. Go ahead. Make your calls."

Leaning in. he brushed her lips with his. "I was supposed to bring you home, make you a nice dinner, see to it you had a relaxing evening."

"Rowan's idea?"

"She thinks so."'

"Make your calls," she said. "It smells like Rowan already started dinner. So while the two of you take care of this crisis, I'll go check on it. Okay?"

He nodded, drew one finger over her lips, and then sighing in regret, turned to finish dialing the phone.

Mirabella found her way to the kitchen on her own. But she felt cold inside despite the heat of the oven. She was on a runaway train, heading straight for disaster, and she was damned if she knew how to stop it in time.

CHAPTER 6

It was after ten by the time Bella finished helping Jonathon clean up from dinner and Rowan was settled into her bed, sleeping restlessly.

She sat beside him now, on a wicker love seat on the deck in back. Stars glittered by the thousands from a clear deep blue sky, and she wondered how death could lurk so near on such a beautiful night. The moon was nearly full, and it bore a rose-colored halo this night. That gave Mirabella pause. Her mother used to call that a Witch Moon, because of the red garter the moon appeared to wear. In some traditions, the red garter was still a symbol of the Craft. Bella's mother always said a red-ringed moon meant an added boost to a Witch's magickal powers. But others called that ruby halo "blood on the moon" and took it as a bad omen. A sign of danger.

Bella didn't know which belief was correct. Maybe both. Maybe the added danger made the boost of power necessary. Maybe that was why they came as one.

"You could stay, you know," Jonathon said softly.

She drew her gaze from the moon to look into his eyes.

"I didn't mean.... " He swallowed hard. "We have guest rooms."

She nodded. "If I stay I won't be in any guest room, Jonathon. And I think after what happened between us this afternoon, we both know it. Besides, I have some things I need to do tonight," she said, keeping her tone level with effort. It was difficult, out here, alone with him like this. She was finding herself more and more drawn to this man with every moment she spent near him. And that was dangerous. She knew it too well.

"Did I scare you off with that...that kiss?"

She lowered her head. "It was a little more than a kiss. If Rowan hadn't called, I...." She lowered her head, licked her lips. In her mind she saw them tearing at each other's clothes in her back yard. Making love, standing up, in broad daylight. It had been that frantic what had happened between them.

"I wish she hadn't called," he said, and his voice was coarse.

She lifted her head. His face was close. He bent to her, kissed her. And that heat began uncoiling inside her all over again.

He slid his mouth from hers, over her jaw, and to the tender skin of her neck. Bella tipped her head back and curled her fingers in his hair. His lips, his mouth and teeth on her skin...it was too good. Too wonderful to resist.

"I'll slow down if that's what you want." He murmured, lifting his head. His hand was at her blouse, his fingers fumbling with the buttons. "But tell me now." A button came loose. She didn't say anything. He undid another. And then his hand slipped inside her blouse, and inside her bra, and closed around her breast. His breath stuttered out of him as she sucked hers in at his touch. Callused skin. Warm and rough. "You're not saying anything," he whispered. He drew his thumb and forefinger together on her nipple.

So she said something. She said, "Do that again."

His smile was slow and deliciously devilish. He pinched again, harder this time, and she arched against him. He took her mouth, tugging the rest of the buttons free, and pushing the blouse aside. He took her bra off her, and bent to use his mouth where his hand had been. And it was such sweet torment to feel him suckling her, nipping and pulling as if he'd eat her alive.

He pulled her to the deck with him, pulled her down on top of him, and he was inside her.

Just that suddenly. They were one. Mirabella tipped her head back and rocked her body over his. And she knew in that instant just before she lost herself again to sensation, she knew that this was not simply sex. She was linked to this man. He would be her lover, or her executioner, her salvation or her ruin. Nothing in between.

She cried his name and fell against his chest. And he held her so gently, so lovingly.

"God, Mirabella, where the hell did you come from? How can this be?" he whispered into her hair. "How can it be?"

She kissed his neck, and his ear. "Our souls have danced before, Jonathon. And will again. What you feel right now is real. Hold onto it. Please."

Lifting her head slowly, she stared into his eyes, trying to see into his soul. "This...is real. Our souls know each other very well. But now...now we have to come back to the place we call reality the rest of the time. That place where you don't know me at all, and where you may not like me very much when you do."

"Not possible," he whispered. "Mirabella, I...."

"Shhh." She pressed a finger to his lips. "We need to talk, Jonathon."

Gently, she kissed his mouth, then she got off him, and slowly fixed her clothes, buttoned her blouse. He did likewise, though she could see he didn't want to. She sat on the wicker love seat, and he sat down beside her.

"Okay, mysterious Mirabella," he said, his tone loving, teasing. "What don't I know about you? You're beautiful. You're special. There's something about you that draws me like magic, Mirabella. And you love Rowan. A blind man could see that."

"It's true. I do love her. I'd risk my life for her."

He smiled at her, reaching out to straighten her hair. "I know that. You already have, as a matter of fact."

"And maybe I still am."

His brows bent until they touched. "What do you mean?"

She gave her head a rapid shake. "Will you tell me something, Jonathon?"

"Anything. Just ask."

She nodded. "Why do you hate anything having to do with Witchcraft so much?"

His face changed. The gentleness faded, and a hint of harshness came in its place. His jaw went tight, his eyes, narrow. "Why do you ask?"

Bella lifted both brows. "You said you'd tell me anything. So tell me this. Your wife was a Witch, wasn't she?"

He sent her a swift, searching look, and for the first time she saw his eyes cloud with suspicion. "How do you know that?"

"Rowan told me."

His eyes went wider. "Then she knows?"

"Yes. She knows. And she knows you disapprove of it, and refuse to talk about it, and try to keep it secret from her."

"Wait a minute, wait a minute." He gave his head a shake. Bella...have you been talking to my daughter about...about Witchcraft?"

Bella swallowed hard. "Rowan asked me if her mother was the kind of person who went around butchering helpless animals and defacing tombstones with their blood."

He lowered his head slowly, pressing his palms to his forehead. "I didn't ask you what she talked about, Bella. I asked what you told her."

She drew a breath. "Well, what do you think I told her?" she asked. "I mean, for God's sake, Jonathon. Was she?"

"Was who, what?"

"Was your wife the kind of person who went around butchering-"

"No!" He shot to his feet as he said it, pacing slowly away. "No," he said more softly. "Ashley wouldn't even kill spiders."

Mirabella watched him and wished she didn't have to put him through this kind of pain, but she didn't have a choice. "What was it about her beliefs that you hated so much? I mean, there had to be something."

He shook his head. "I didn't know much about her beliefs. I didn't want to know." He met Bella's eyes. "And I still don't. It's a lot of ridiculous superstition, hocus-pocus bullshit that weakens minds, makes people believe in the impossible instead of focusing on hard, cold reality."

Bella frowned. "You really believe that?"

He nodded. "Of course I do. And it was my wife who proved it to me beyond any doubt."

Mirabella tilted her head to one side. "How?"

"She died, Bella." He sighed, pushing a hand through his hair. "She had ovarian cancer. She and her crazy friends thought they could beat it, even when the doctors had given up hope. But all their healing spells and chanting and herbal teas and candle burning didn't do a damn bit of good. If there were any such thing as magick or Witchcraft, then how could she have died? How could she possibly have been yanked away from me-from Rowan-so far before her time?"

Bella went to him, touched his face. "My sweet Jonathon...if it was before her time, she wouldn't have gone. She left because she had accomplished what she came into this lifetime to do. Maybe her mission was to give life to Rowan. Maybe she just wanted to experience being loved by a man like you. Or having a daughter, or...no one can say. But she's not really gone. She's only moved on."

He shook his head. "It's smoke and mirrors. Garbage. And now it's being used to twist young minds like that of Bryan Marcomb, and look at the results." He stared at her, shaking his head slowly. "You're a teacher, Mirabella. God, you of all people should know better than to believe in...in Witches, for God's sake."

"It would be awfully hard not to," she said. "Considering I am one."

He slammed his eyes closed, swore under his breath.

Mirabella took a step away from him. "I've kept the truth to myself long enough, Jonathon. Something's going on...something that involves you, and me, and Rowan. And...and maybe Ashley. Now you can believe what you want about me, my spirituality, my powers or lack thereof, but you must know damn well I would never do anything to hurt your daughter." She licked her lips. "She's in danger, Jonathon."

His head came up slowly, eyes narrowing on her. "What kind of danger?"

"The same kind that Bryan Marcomb was in."'

"Suicide?" He gripped her wrists tight. "Suicide? For God's sake! What do you know? And how do you know it? Tell me. Mirabella."

She glanced downward, at where he held her, and he eased his grip, but didn't let go. "I don't know anything. Except that someone is trying to help me protect Rowan.

When that truck almost hit her. I saw a woman, pointing, and I knew what was about to happen."

He frowned. "What...could the truck possibly have to do with-"

"Not the truck. The woman. I think she was Ashley."

He released her wrists as if they'd turned into snakes and would bite him. His lips parted, and his face twisted into a grimace as if he'd just bitten into something sour. "My God. You're right, Mirabella. I don't know you. Not in the least."

She managed not to flinch at his words. She had to get through this, tell him everything. "I've seen her again, too. At my house, standing behind me in the mirror. And Rowan's been seeing her as well."

"Oh, for the love of Christ!" He threw up his hands. "Enough. It's enough. Just stop it."

"She's trying to warn us. Damn it, she'd probably come to you too, if you weren't too closed-minded to let her."

"It's bullshit!"

"Is it?" She drew a breath, sighed deeply. Then lowering her head, shook it from side to side. "I guess it's time I went home." When he started to move, she held up a hand. "No. I'll walk. It's only a few blocks, and...I like the night."

"You shouldn't walk alone."

"I want to. I have a lot of thinking to do. And Jonathon, so do you. Rowan is hurting and confused. Maybe it would be a good idea for you to learn a little bit about what it is you're condemning before you write it off, hmm? For her sake? You don't have to agree with it. You don't have to believe in it. Just respect it for what it is, and know it for what it isn't. Witches don't sacrifice animals, Jonathon. And they don't drive kids to suicide."

He lowered his head. "I know that much."

"Do you? Do you really?" She shook her head slowly, and walked away.

"Bella?"

She turned slowly, looked back at him.

"Why the hell didn't you tell me this before you let me...."

"Let you what? Fall in love with me?" she said. Her voice was soft with unshed tears, but she knew he could hear her. "We've been in love for a long, long time, Jonathon. Before we ever met, I think." She lowered her head. "But you don't believe in that kind of thing, do you?"

Turning, she walked away.

THERE WAS a pall over the entire town as she walked through it to school the next morning. But she stopped, when she saw the bright red spray paint and the broken glass at Gwen's place. Across the front walk in bloody lettering, were the words, "Suffer not a Witch to live."

"Oh no.," Bella whispered as a cold hand closed around her heart. "Oh, Goddess, please, no!" Racing across the street toward the shop with her heart in her throat, she shouted, "Gwen! Gwenyth!"

Gwen came out the door before she even got there. "Oh, thank goodness!" Bella said, grabbing Gwen and hugging her hard, kissing her cheek. "Thank goodness. Are you okay? Hmm?" She backed off, pressing her palms to the sides of Gwen's face. Her cheeks were tear streaked and her eyes, puffy. But she was in one piece, thank the Goddess!

Bella hugged her hard, looking past her at the men in overalls who were chipping the jagged pieces of glass out of the window, preparing to install a new one. Others were just arriving in a pick up truck, and unloading their paint and brushes. "Honey, what happened?"

"Circe's missing," she said, her voice raspy. "I'm so afraid they took her, and I just keep thinking about what's been going on with...with animals around here lately."

"Oh no," Bella whispered. "Come on, come inside, and tell me everything." She kept one arm firmly around Gwen's shoulders as she led her into the shop, through it, and to the small parlor off the back that divided the shop from the rest of the house and served as Gwen's temple room. "Sit," Bella said, pressing her into a chair. "Now talk."

Gwen lugged a tissue from her pocket and swiped at her face. "It must've been around three a.m. I heard the glass breaking. I came downstairs. The window was smashed, there was a brick on the floor." She shook her head slowly. "And I couldn't find Circe, so I went outside, calling, her and that's when I saw the paint on the front wall." She shuddered with her whole body at the memory. "I thought it was blood at first...."

"Did you call the police?"

"Yes. They're calling it vandalism."

Bella frowned. "Vandalism? This is a hate crime!"

Gwen frowned, shaking her head slowly. "This is it, Bella. I can't take it anymore. I think I'm going to go ahead and take Mark Hayes' offer on the house."

"But you can't. This was your great-grandmother's legacy. Oh. Gwen, please think this over some more."

Gwen lowered her head.

"Look, at least don't make any decisions right now. "Not when you're still this upset."

She sniffled, nodded. "I'm not going anywhere until I find out what happened to Circe, at least."

"I'm sure she just got scared by the noise and ran off to hide. She'll show up soon." She reached across the table to clasp Gwen's hands. "You want me to make you some tea?"

"No. I'm fine, really. You...probably need to go."

Bella glanced at her watch. "I have another minute or two."

"Liar." Gwen said, dashing her eyes dry. "So how are things going with the prosecutor and his daughter?"

Bella pursed her lips and shook her head. "Well, his first wife was a Witch. He seems to think that because she died of ovarian cancer, that's some kind of proof that the entire belief system is bogus. And, he knows that includes me."

"You told him?" Gwen asked, wide eyed.

"I had to." She shook her head. "His wife's name was Ashley. And I'm pretty sure I've had a couple of visitations from her. So has Rowan."

Gwen lifted her brows. "She's trying to drive you away?"

"No. I don't think so. She's trying to help me protect Rowan from...whatever the hell is about to happen to her."

"Then you have an ally."

"A powerful one, I think," Bella said.

Gwen smiled. "Well, if you see Witch Ashley again, would you ask her to look out for Circe, maybe send her home if she sees her?"

"Maybe you'll be able to ask her yourself. If you're up to a full blown ritual."

Gwen lifted her brows. "You want to try to stir her spirit, see if we can get some answers?"

"Yeah, and I'm thinking it might take the full coven to do it."

"We should have been working on uncovering the truth behind what's been going on in this town before now," Gwen said. "But everyone's been too damned scared of being found out to come to circle." She nodded. "But they'll come now. When and where, hon?"

"Tonight. The full moon's in Saturn. Couldn't be much better timing." Bella frowned. "Are you *sure* you're up to this?"

"You bet I am." Gwen tried a shaky smile. "In fact, it's good to have something to focus on besides worrying about my precious feline. Go on, now. You'd better get to work before they fire you."

If only Bella had known how prophetic Gwen's parting words had been.

CHAPTER 7

Mirabella walked into the school building, and knew immediately the place was deserted. Of students at least. An empty school had a feel to it that was different from anything else. Even a *nearly* empty one tended to exude a lonely, haunted feeling.

"Ms. Saint Angeline?"

Mirabella turned her head sharply at the echoing voice and saw Sally Hayes standing in the open doorway of her office.

"Would you come into my office please?"

The woman turned before Mirabella could even answer, stepping back into her office, leaving the door open, leaving Bella no doubt she had just been summoned. A tiny shiver wandered up her spine. She knew beyond any doubt that this was not good.

Standing just inside the office doorway, she said. "Where are all the students?"

"We decided to cancel classes for today," Sally said. "Because of Bryan Marcomb's death. We felt the kids would need a day to deal with the shock. Tomorrow we'll have counselors on hand to help them talk through it."

Bella frowned. She hadn't had the TV or radio on this morning, so she hadn't heard the announcement that school was canceled. But she should have heard it, anyway. Staff were supposed to be notified by phone.

"No one called," she said. "What happened to the telephone tree? Someone cut it down?"

"We didn't call you because we wanted to meet with you this morning, Ms. Saint Angeline."

Bella frowned at the cool, formal tone. "Since when did we stop being on a first name basis, Sally?" Then she looked past her at the closed door to the meeting room, just off this one. "And what do you mean, 'we'?"

Sally Hayes opened the meeting room door. "The school board," she said.

Beyond the door, Mirabella saw the members of the school board seated around a rectangular table. She knew these people. But she'd never feared them. Today they wore the grim, stony faces of a Puritan tribunal, and she felt more than a little bit afraid.

Frowning and fighting the chill that raced up her spine, Bella went inside. Sally Hayes came behind her, closing the door. "I think you know everyone," she said. "Please, have a seat." She indicated one of the two empty chairs at the table. She took the other, at the table's head.

Mirabella sat down. "Fine. I'll play. What's this all about?"

"Ms. Staint Angeline, we have reason to believe that you are involved in the practice of the occult."

"*What?*"

"This emergency meeting of the board has been called in order to give you the chance to defend yourself against these accusations, and so that we may decide what action we need to take for the best interests of the students."

Bella looked slowly around the table. Not one of those present had the gumption to look her in the eye. Her hands shook where they lay flat on the table, and her voice shook when she spoke. "Wicca is a recognized religion in this country, and this state, with all the legal rights entitled to any other religion."

"The occult has been connected to a rash of vicious crimes in our town, Ms. Saint Angeline. Animals tortured and mutilated, vandalism and defacing of property, and most recently, it's been linked to the death of one of our own students. This is a serious cause for concern."

"There is no evidence whatsoever that any of the things you just named are connected to the practice of Witchcraft."

Sally Hayes' perfectly plucked eyebrows rose. "Well now, Bella, what are we supposed to think? That it's the local Baptists out there killing house cats in the graveyards in the dead of night?"

"That would be almost as ridiculous as assuming it was the local Witches," Bella said. But though she tried to sound brave, all she could see in her mind was the dream. The townspeople standing around her, condemning her, watching her burn.

The principal seemed taken aback, but only for a moment. She recovered quickly, and said, "We're not here to determine who was or was not responsible for the crimes in town. We're here to determine whether or not, you, Ms. Saint Angeline, are a member of any occult group or organization."

Mirabella said nothing.

"Well?" the woman prompted. "Do you consider yourself to be...a Witch?" she said the last with a tone of derision, her words dripping sarcasm.

Mirabella looked her in the eye. "Keep fucking with me, Sally, and you're liable to find out."

An audible gasp went up from the people at the table. She knew damn well she should have held her temper. But Witch or not, she was only human. And this was illegal, immoral, and ludicrous. Bella got to her feet. "I'm a Wiccan, a Witch, a Pagan. It's legal. You cannot discipline me for practicing my religion. And I'm not even certain you can legally ask me about it."

"We can however, discipline you for speaking to your students about that so-called religion," Sally said. "Have you been doing that?"

"Of course not!" she blurted, almost before she thought about it. Then she frowned. "Not on school grounds and not in my capacity as a teacher."

"But you have mentioned Witchcraft to students, haven't you?"

She drew a deep, slow breath. "If a student asked me flat out if I were Wiccan, I may have answered yes. I certainly wouldn't have lied. If they asked what that meant, I might have given them a basic, honest answer. That's all."

Mrs. Hayes smiled slowly. "That's all we need."

"What do you mean?"

"Mirabella Saint Angeline, you are hereby suspended without pay from your duties as a teacher at Ezra High School, and forbidden to set foot on the premises, pending a full investigation of your behavior."

"You can't do this." Bella whispered.

"We just did. We will need to formalize this with a vote, of course. But at this point, that's a technicality. It will be unanimous. Go to your classroom, gather your things, and go home."

ROWAN GLANCED at the newspaper for the tenth time.

Jonathon knew the headline by heart. "Local Teacher Suspended on Charges of Witchcraft" He'd tried to trash the evening edition before his daughter caught sight of it, but she'd snagged it from his hand the minute he started for the fireplace with it. Almost as if she were reading his mind.

"Dad, we have to do something," she said.

He'd been thinking the same thing. The question was, what? He'd insulted Bella last night, called her most cherished beliefs so much bullshit. He doubted she would want his help. And even if she did, he wasn't sure what he could do.

"I'll try calling her again."

"Good."

He went to the phone, dialed the number, once again getting a busy signal for his trouble. He hung up. "Still busy."

"That's over an hour. Something's wrong."

He smoothed his daughter's hair. "Hon, don't jump to conclusions. She may have been getting some phone calls she didn't want. She probably took it off the hook."

Rowan grimaced. "Yeah, I can just imagine the kinds of phone calls she was probably getting."

He could too. And he didn't like what he was imagining.

"We should go over there, Dad."

"Honey...." He pushed a hand through his hair. "I just don't think...."

Rowan tipped her head to one side, searching his face with her laser beam eyes that were so much like her mother's it was uncanny. "Tell me the truth. Why don't you want to go over? No...you *do* want to go, don't you? You just don't want *me* to go."

He sighed. He couldn't lie to this kid. It just wasn't possible. "I'd rather not drag you into something until I'm sure of the situation. I don't know what's going on over there right now, and-"

"And you're overprotective and hyper to boot. Fine. I'll stay home. Just so long as someone goes over."

"I'm not real comfortable leaving you here alone either, with all that's been going on."

The doorbell rang. Sighing and rolling her eyes, Rowan went to get it. And when she came back, she had her best friend Shauna at her side. Shauna looked old, for a teenager. Dark circles under her eyes and a washed-out look to her face. Poor kid. This hadn't been easy on her.

"Shauna wants to hang out here tonight, okay, Dad?"

"Sure. How are you. Shauna?" He kept his voice soft.

"I'm gonna be all right, Mr. Hawthorne. I just wish it would stop hurting."

He reached out a hand to stroke the girl's hair. "It eases up in time. After awhile, you'll be able to remember the good times and even smile a little. I promise."

She looked up at him. "I guess if you can say that, then I have to believe it."

"It doesn't feel like it right now though," he said. "I know."

"Dad, why don't you go now? I won't be home alone, and Shauna and I will be fine."

He looked from one of them to the other. "You sure?"

"Yeah. We'll eat some junk food and talk it out."

He bit his lower lip. During the course of the investigation of her boyfriend, Shauna had been checked out, and there hadn't been any indication that she'd been involved in or even aware of Bryan's questionable activities. Hell, they never really found proof that he'd done anything more than be in the wrong place at the wrong time.

And Jonathon really *did* want to check on Bella.

And it was *only* a few blocks away.

"Okay." he said at last. "Okay, but don't go anywhere. And call if you need me. All right?"

"Sure," Rowan said.

"Thanks, Mr. Hawthorne," Shauna said in her hoarse-from-crying voice.

Jonathon left the girls and drove over to Mirabella's house. When he got there, though, he wished he'd come sooner.

A crowd had gathered outside. Angry locals and reporters. He couldn't have walked through them to the front door if he'd wanted to. But he didn't see Bella's car in the driveway anyway. She usually walked everywhere she went, if it was local. Probably, though, walking wasn't the safest prospect for her right at the moment.

His throat went a little dry.

He drove on past and tried to think where she might go, when she had every reason to doubt her welcome at any place in this town. Including his own.

Only one answer came to mind.

So he drove there. To that little shop that had been vandalized the night before. He'd heard about it at work.

And her car was there. But the place was dark as a dungeon.

Frowning Jonathon parked across the street, got out, and went over to the shop's front door. The town was dead tonight. Everyone was either shouting obscenities outside Bella's house or at the school gym for the town meeting that had been called to address the problem of Witchcraft in Ezra Township. He'd heard a rumor they'd located an old law on the books which made teaching Witchcraft to a minor a criminal act, with no maximum sentence. It had to have been left over from the seventeenth century when the town was first founded. Now some wanted to resurrect it, enforce it, and prosecute those who'd broken it.

He crossed the sidewalk and stared up at the old Victorian house. The front wall still smelled of new paint, and the window had been replaced. No lettering on it yet, though.

A soft sound drifted up from below, and something bunted his leg. He glanced down to see a black cat rubbing against him.

"Hey, you wouldn't be the missing Circe, would you?" He bent down. There was a tag dangling from the cat's collar, and he bet it had a name on it. He would like to be able to return one missing pet to its owner intact.

But when he reached for the cat, she dodged him, and trotted around the house. Frowning, he went after her. She didn't go far. In fact, after a few yards, she turned to look back and waited for him to catch up.

When he did, she didn't run off again. Just stood still and let him scoop her up. He glanced at the tag...then turned his head slowly.

The haunting sound of voices, chanting in an overlapping, ever changing cadence, caught his attention. He looked at the windows, where the sound seemed to come from, and saw the flickering dance of candlelight casting shadows. Shapes of women, moving.

And there was a door...and oddly, it was open.

He held the cat close, and silently, drawn in spite of himself, he went through the door into a back room of the house.

CHAPTER 8

Rowan and Shauna sat in Rowan's bedroom, nibbling ice cream out of the carton. They reclined side by side on the bed, and the stereo played Seether.

For an hour, Shauna had been pouring her heart out about Bryan. How much she'd loved him. How much she was going to miss him. And crying.

She'd been crying a lot.

Rowan just listened and didn't worry about saying the right thing, because as Bella had told her, there really was no right thing. And she thought Bella was right.

Talking it out did seem to be easing Shauna's mind a little bit. It made Rowan feel she was helping her, in some small way.

And then, out of the blue. Shauna said. "I just wish he'd never got involved with that whole mess. I mean, it wasn't worth it. It just screwed up his head."

Rowan tried not to look as alarmed as she felt. "What whole mess, Shauna?"

Shauna sniffled, wiped her eyes. "Nothing. I mean...I don't

want his name being dragged through the mud, Rowan. He's gone now, you know? It would be too hard on his mom."

"I wouldn't want his mom to suffer any more than she already has. Or you either. Come on. I'm your best friend. If you don't get it out, it's just gonna keep eating at you until you do, you know."

Shauna blinked her red-rimmed eyes. "It has been helping, talking to you. How'd you get so smart anyway?"

"Mirabella-Miss Saint A, I mean. She told me you were going to need friends who'd just let you spill it all out."

Shauna lowered her head. "I guess Miss Saint A's going through some garbage of her own right now, huh?"

"They suspended her from her job at school. It's all over the papers that she's some kind of cat-murdering devil-worshiper."

"That's so lame." Shauna said. "They're so stupid. She's the best teacher we ever had."

"I know."

"She wouldn't hurt a freaking fly, you know?"

"I know."

Drawing a breath. Shauna lifted her chin. "Rowan, Miss Saint A didn't have anything to do with those animals they've been finding all cut up."

"I know."

"Yeah, but...I mean. I *really* know it."

Rowan frowned. "How?"

"Because...it was Bryan, and a couple of other guys. Swear you won't tell!"

Rowan heard what she said, but it took an extra beat to sink in. It was that far beyond belief. When she could finally spit out words, she blurted, "Why the hell would he *do* something like that?"

"Because he was paid to."

Rowan frowned hard, and tipped her head sideways. "You

mean it didn't have anything to do with any...occult stuff at all?"

"No, of course not. Bryan's only religion was football and that stupid old junk car he wanted to re-build. He was getting paid a lot, Rowan. I mean, it was nothing for him to have three or four hundred bucks on him all at once. When he started throwing all that cash around, I thought...I don't know, I thought he was dealing drugs or something. So he told me the truth. Someone was paying him a ton of money to kidnap cats and rabbits and stuff, and cut them up and leave them where they would be found. The guy gave him instructions too. How he had to make symbols in blood and stuff. It was disgusting."

"Jeez, Shauna! What were you thinking? Why didn't you say something?"

She looked shocked at Rowan's anger. "Hey, don't act like I'm the one who was killing animals!"

Rowan just looked at her.

Shauna lowered her head. "Bryan hated it. I mean, he felt awful about it. And he said he never tortured anything, like the papers say. He always killed them first, before any of the —other stuff. And he promised me he'd stop. Then the cops saw him that last night in the cemetery. And he got scared. He told the guy he was working for that he wanted no more to do with it. He wanted out, you know?"

"Yeah?" By now, Rowan was facing her on the bed, gripping her hands hard, eager to hear more. "And then what happened?"

"Nothing. The guy said fine, no problem. Bryan seemed so relieved. I thought he was gonna be okay, you know?" Shauna lowered her head as tears welled up again. "I guess he just couldn't deal with the guilt of killing those innocent animals, though."

"Right. Bryan killed himself over some cats and bunnies."

Shauna burst into noisy tears, and Rowan hugged her and rubbed her shoulders while she cried. "I'm sorry. I shouldn't have said that, but don't you see how ridiculous it is? Shauna, you have to tell me something." She pushed Shauna back a bit, so she could look her in the eye. "Who was the guy paying Bryan and the others to do this stuff?"

Shauna shrugged. "Bryan didn't tell me."

"Well, we have to find out."

"Row! You promised you wouldn't tell anyone!"

Rowan gaped. "Hello? Shauna, are you telling me you still don't get it? Think, will you? Bryan is questioned by the cops. Then he tells this jerk he wants out, and twenty-four hours later, Bryan is dead. Doesn't that make you wonder, even a little bit, Shauna? Doesn't it?"

Shauna frowned. Then slowly her brows rose, her eyes widened, and her face went even whiter. "Oh my God...do you think...?"

"I don't know. But I think we'd better find out. Don't you?"

"I said all along Bryan would never kill himself! God, Rowan, what are we gonna do?"

"We have to find out who the guy was. Maybe the other kids involved would talk. Did Bryan say-?"

"No. No, he wouldn't tell me any details." She licked her lips, eyed Rowan. "Maybe there's something in Bryan's room. I mean, he kept journals-and I think this guy e-mailed him too. We could check his computer." Then she lowered her head. "But the cops have probably already done all that."

'"No. No, it was ruled a suicide and blamed on Witchcraft. They didn't dig too much farther once all that was decided. Will his mom let us in his room?" Rowan asked. She seriously doubted it.

"She's not home. My mom took her out. She...she wanted a new suit for Bryan to wear for...for the funeral. She just couldn't bear to do it alone. That's why I came over. I couldn't make myself go with them, but I didn't want to be alone either."

She started to cry again.

Rowan gripped her shoulders. "I know. It's awful, I know. But come on now, pull it together, Shauna. Get a grip. For Bryan."

Sniffling, Shauna nodded, got hold of herself.

"Can we get in, Shauna? Can we get into Bryan's house, his room?"

"Yeah," she whispered. "He always left his window-unlatched, in case I wanted to come by to say goodnight."

Rowan nodded, even though that sentence had her tearing up almost as much as Shauna was. "All right," she said. "Okay then. Listen, I can do this myself if you're not up for it."

Shauna dashed the back of her hand across her eyes, and got to her feet. "I'm in. If someone killed Bryan, I damn well want to know who."

They grabbed jackets, flashlights, and they headed out into the night. But when they got to Bryan's house, someone else was already there.

JONATHON WALKED SILENTLY into the large room, the cat nestled in his arms. A group of women stood in a circle, holding hands, and they didn't even notice him there. They were faces he knew. Granny Kate. Dr. Plummer. One of the secretaries from the DA's office, for crying out loud.

Mirabella was in the center of the circle. And he'd never seen her look like she did then. Her dress was simple, white, draping, tied with a braided cord of three colors. Her hair hung loosely down her back. She wore several necklaces, all of them laden with gemstones. Amber and jet. Moonstone and citrine. Others he couldn't have named. She stood with eyes closed, head tipped slightly back, arms up and out to the sides. The candlelight painted her face. And in spite of himself, he thought she looked more beautiful than any woman he'd ever set eyes on.

The other women chanted, their song falling into so many layers of harmony he couldn't separate one from another. It was beautiful. They sang the names of ancient Goddesses, and he thought he heard the sea, but there was no source for that. The smoke of incense filled the air. And there was something else. Something different about the space in the room where he stood, and the space within that circle of female bodies. That circle was different somehow, denser or...or something.

But then he couldn't focus on that, either, because the chanting stopped all at once, and Mirabella turned to her left and spoke, but her voice was different, deeper, richer, almost ethereal.

"Ashley Rowan Hawthorne, I stir thy spirit! Come ye forth, from beyond the Western gate! Bring thy message now! For the sake of thy daughter, come!"

And the others began to chant again, only this time it was his dead wife's name they sang. Over and over again, they said it.

Tears boiled from Jonathon's eyes, rolling down his face. He opened his mouth to shout at them, to forbid this nonsense. But before he could utter a sound, he saw something. A swirl of particles, dust motes or atoms, gathered like a misty whirlwind right in front of Mirabella. And when they solidified, she was standing there. Ashley. She was filmy, and thin, but there.

Jonathon whispered her name in a harsh voice and lunged forward. But he hit some invisible barrier when he would have forced himself between the women in the circle. Some shield that wasn't solid, but pressed him back all the same.

Mirabella's eyes were still closed. But she drew her hands in, turned her palms out, and as Jonathon stared in wide-eyed wonder. Ashley pressed her misty hands flat to Bella's.

"What do you want me to do?" Bella asked.

"Love her." It was a long drawn out whisper, like the sound of a breeze in treetops.

"I *do* love her."'

"Save her." Ashley whispered, long and slowly.

"How?"

Ashley's arms slid around Bella. It looked as intimate as an embrace between sisters. But he could see...or sense...her lips moving near Bella's ear. And then there was a wind, so strong it sent the door banging against the wall behind him. The candles went out in a whoosh. The cat leapt out of his arms.

He couldn't see Ashley or Bella any more, and frantically, he searched for the light switch, and found it.

With a flick of his hand, the room was flooded with light. Bella was sitting on the floor, shaking her head as if stunned. Gwenyth, the blond who owned the shop, stooped as the cat ran to her, and she scooped the animal up with a shout of joy.

Bella got to her feet, saw him, and started forward, looking dazed.

"Cut a door!" someone yelled, and the woman in front of Bella traced an arch in the air.

Bella moved through it, and straight to Jonathon.

"What the hell just happened here?" he asked, and his voice was strained to the point where he could barely form audible words.

"We have to go. We have to go to Rowan."

He barely heard her. He was still staring at the spot where he'd seen Ashley. "Was that...how could she...*Ashley's dead....* "

"There's no such thing as dead."

"But...but...."

She slapped him. Her palm was hot, he noticed, and it didn't sting much. Just enough to make him focus on her.

"Rowan is in trouble. We have to go. *Now.*" She spoke with authority and power he'd sensed in her, but never seen before. And he found himself believing every word.

He nodded, still too stunned to speak. Mirabella took his hand firmly in hers and pulled him along toward the door. Over her shoulder she called, "Take up the circle. Call the police and send them to Bryan Marcomb's house. And hurry."

And the next thing Jonathon knew he was being tugged out the door, around the house to the driveway where her car was parked. She opened the passenger door and shoved him into the scat. Then she went to her side and got behind the wheel. A second later, they were speeding through town.

CHAPTER 9

Rowan was standing outside Bryan's house, pushing up his bedroom window with Shauna tight to her side when she saw something moving inside the room.

She went stiff and still.

"What?" Shauna whispered.

Rowan backed up, pulling Shauna with her. "Someone's in there."

"Did they see you?"

"I don't know. I don't—" The window was yanked open, and a dark form filled it "—Think so," Rowan finished.

The two girls turned to run, but Rowan could hear the footfalls behind them. And in less than a second, a big hand hit her hard, right between the shoulder blades, and sent her face-first into the ground.

She rolled over onto her back, crab walking backwards from the man looming over her.

"Mr. Hayes," she panted. "What are you...why are you—?"

Shauna screamed for all she was worth, and Rowan

looked toward her, only to see Mrs. Hayes, their own high school principal grabbing hold of her.

The man reached for Rowan, and she flung up a hand like a stop sign. She didn't know what made her do it, but every part of her was focused on one thing. Pushing him away from her. And though she never touched him, he went backward, staggering, then falling. She scrambled to her feet, turned to run, and hit a solid chest.

JONATHON SAW his daughter send the attacker stumbling backward. And sure, he might have tripped, or just lost his balance. But he didn't think so.

He and Mirabella had sped straight here, heard Shauna's scream, and ran like the wind into the backyard just in time to see Hayes fall on his ass. Then Rowan was on her feet, turning to run. And then she was in her father's arms.

She jerked back, doubling up a fist and raising it. Then she blinked at him and hurled herself against him all over again. "Daddy!"

Beside him, Mirabclla was holding a shaken Shauna, calming her. Sirens wailed, not that the police were overly called for. A coven of Witches had thundered into the yard only a minute behind him and Bella, their robes dancing in the night wind, their hair smelling of sandalwood. Several of them were hauling Mr. Hayes to his feet, while a handful of others were busily subduing Mrs. Hayes, who had released Shauna and tried to run for it.

Officer Billy Cantone came running. He took in the women, most of whom he knew, all of whom were dressed in ritual robes and jewelry, many of whom wore five pointed stars on chains. "Just what the hell is going on here?"

Mirabella stepped forward. "I think I can answer that. Mr.

and Mrs. Hayes have been very eager to purchase my friend Gwenyth's house, on the edge of town. You know the one? Mr. Hayes has Gwen's permission to fish in the stream out back. And he made his first offer shortly after she first gave him that permission, this spring. He wanted the house very badly. Didn't you. Mr. Hayes?"

He grunted, and looked away.

"She turned him down. So he decided to get her run out of town. And since she was openly Wiccan, what better way to do that than to orchestrate a few ritualistic animal sacrifices, get the locals all stirred up over the Witches in their midst? Hmm?"

Sniffling, young Shauna lifted her head. "You were the one paying Bryan Marcomb to kill those animals that way, mess up the tombstones, and all that?"

"You bet he was," Rowan said. "And when Bryan wanted out-threatened to tell the police everything unless you let him go, you killed him. Didn't you?"

Jonathon stroked his daughter's hair. "And then you came back here to get rid of any evidence of a connection between you and Bryan," he said, as his mind filled in the blanks.

"My God. Is this all true?" Officer Cantone asked.

"I'm sure we'll find the evidence, either on these two, or still in Bryan's room." Jonathon said. "But what I don't understand is why? Why is one piece of property worth more than a young boy's life? Hmm?"

"It's the pyrite in the stream out behind the house." Mirabella said softly. She walked over to where her friend Gwenyth stood looking puzzled. "It's not really pyrite at all, hon. It's the real thing. Gold. And Jim Hayes knew it. And he wanted it all for himself."

The cop's eyes widened. "How do you know all that, Miss Saint Angeline?"

She looked at Jonathon. And he knew. He knew these

were the things that his wife had whispered to her in that magickal circle. How else could she have figured it all out-or known to come here, now, just at the moment when his daughter's life was in grave danger?

"An old friend told me," Mirabella said softly. "She, uh, prefers her name be kept out of this. It's nothing you can't verify, after all."

"Arrest those two, Billy." Jonathon instructed. "And get some men out here to go through Bryan's room for evidence. We'll take the witnesses' statements tomorrow. It's been...a long night."

Billy cuffed Mark and Sally Hayes, and escorted them to the waiting cruiser. Mirabella turned to Jonathon, to Rowan. "It's done." And then she turned, and walked away.

THERE WAS no doubt in Bella's mind that, given the chance, the Hayes couple would have taken Rowan, and perhaps Shauna as we'll, killed them, and tried to make it look like suicide. Or maybe an accident. And if they had succeeded, it would have been one more crime for the good folk of Ezra Township to lay at the feet of the local Witches. And possibly, at Bella's own feet.

But thanks to one determined mother's love for her daughter, it didn't turn out that way.

Bella got all the way to her car. The others were pulling away now. The police car. The vehicles of her friends and sisters. She stood there, listening to the motors fade in the distance. Then to the crickets chirping and the gentle breeze whispering through the trees.

And then the breeze changed. It whispered "Mirabella..." in a voice that was becoming familiar.

Ashley's voice.

Closing her eyes to prevent tears, Bella said, "I saved her. What more do you want from me?"

"Save *him*...." the trees seemed to whisper.

Bella opened her eyes, a trill of alarm running up her spine. "How?"

"Love him."

Damn. Why did her heart have to hurt so much? "I already do," she said softly, and she turned, and he was standing there.

"I'm sorry," Jonathon said. "I was wrong. I was wrong about everything. I was wrong about your faith, your beliefs. I was wrong about Ashley and about my own daughter. But most of all, Bella, I was wrong to ever let myself think for one minute that I had any choice at all about loving you. Because I didn't. And I don't."

She lifted her brows, tipped her head back to search his face.

"I need you," he told her.

Beside him, Rowan said, "We both do."

Bella blinked as her eyes filled with tears. "I...I don't know what to say."

"Say you'll marry me." Jonathon said.

Rowan clasped her hands together, pursing her lips and blinking her own tears back as she waited to hear Bella's answer. She might even have been holding her breath.

Mirabella smiled. "I'll marry you."

He swept her into his arms, and kissed her deeply. And then they parted just enough to enfold Rowan in their arms as well.

"Take care of each other," the breeze whispered.

Rowan pulled free of them, and looked up toward the sky. "We will, Mom. Thank you. Thank you for sending Mirabella to me."

Bella, arm in arm with Jonathon, went to her. "Don't

think she won't be back, just because this little crisis is over," Bella said softly. "She'll always be with you, Rowan. And so will I."

Jonathon shook his head. Rowan and Bella both looked at him, and he had tears in his eyes. "I don't know what I ever did to deserve to have three such incredible women in my life." His voice was choked with emotion. "But I'm so glad I did it, whatever it was." He looked at Rowan. "Because I love you. I love you so much." And then he turned to Bella, cupping her face in his hands. "And you...you saved my heart. My soul. You made me live again. I didn't think I could love this way twice in a lifetime. But Bella, I do. And I believe you, what you said before. This isn't the first time around for us."

"No, it isn't," she told him. "And it isn't going to be the last."

-THE END-

Read a sample of Maggie's full length, epic, first-in-series novel, ETERNITY.

"A hauntingly beautiful story of a love that endures through time itself." –NYT Bestselling author Kay Hooper

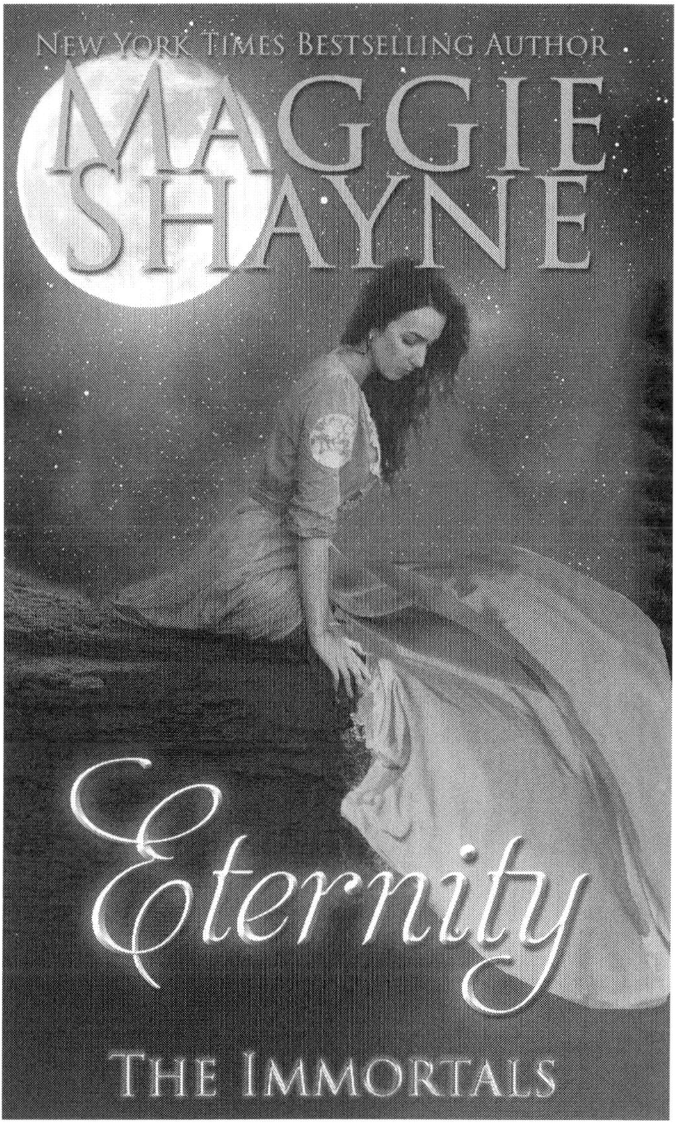
NEW YORK TIMES BESTSELLING AUTHOR
MAGGIE
SHAYNE
Eternity
THE IMMORTALS

EXCERPT: ETERNITY

I always knew I was a witch.

The definition of the word has since broadened somewhat, and rightly so, I imagine. Today anyone with the determination to learn and practice the Craft of the Wise can call herself—and deservedly—a witch. But in my time there were no books written to guide a seeker, save the books of the witches themselves, but the grimoires were kept secret. Back then one was only a witch if one was born to, or adopted by, another witch. And even then the young one wasn't told all of the secrets. Some of them I didn't learn until much later.

My mother was a wise woman, a witch, and from the time I was very young I was taught the ways of drawing on the power of the sun and the moon and the stars and of nature itself. Above all else, I was taught the importance of keeping all that I learned secret. For the penalty meted out to practitioners of the Craft in those days was harsh. Mother never told me just how harsh. I learned that when I was twenty and one, in a lesson so cruel its memory remains burned in my mind, though three full centuries have passed.

And yet it was because of that cruelty that I first set eyes upon Duncan Wallace.

The key to my mother's ruin was her kindness. My father had died only a fortnight before, of a plague her simple folk magic could not fight. Many lives were lost in our small English village that brutal winter of 1689, and perhaps my mother simply could not bear to see one more death after so much grief.

At any rate, it was Matilda, the sister of my dead father, who came pounding on our door that dark wintry night. Looking startled at Aunt Matilda's state—wild hair and wilder eyes and not so much as a cloak about her shoulders—Mother drew her inside and bade her take the rocking chair beside the hearth to warm herself. I offered tea to calm her. But Aunt Matilda seemed crazed and refused to sit down. Instead, she paced in agitated strides, her skirts swishing about her legs, her thin slippers leaving damp footprints on our wood floor.

"No time to sit an' sip tea," she told us. "Not now. 'Tis my youngest, my little Johnny, named for my own dear brother who has gone to his reward. My Johnny has taken ill!" She whirled and grabbed my mother, gripping the front of her dress in white-knuckled fists. "I know you can help him. *I know,* I tell you! An' if you refuse me now, Lily St. James, I vow—"

"Matilda, calm yourself!" My mother's firm voice quieted the woman, though only for a moment, I feared. "I would never refuse to help Johnny in any way I can. You know that."

"I *don't* know it!" my aunt shrieked. "Not when you let your own husband die of the same ailment! Pray, Lily, why didn't you save him? Why didn't you save my brother?"

My mother's head lowered, and I saw the pain flare anew in her eyes—a pain that sometimes dulled but never died away.

"I tried everything I knew to help Jonathon. But I couldn't save him," she whispered.

"Perhaps because you brought the illness on him from the start."

"Aunt Matilda!" I stepped between the two, forgetting to respect my elders and tugging my aunt's arm until she faced me, rather than my mother. "You know better. My parents shared a love such as few people ever know, and I'll not stand by and hear you sully its memory."

"Raven, don't," Mother began.

But I rushed on. "No one can bring on such a plague as this, and well you know it!"

"No one but a witch, you mean, don't you, Raven? *Raven.* She even named you for some dark carrion bird. Are you practicing the black arts as well, girl?" Aunt Matilda gripped my shoulders, shook me. "Are you? *Are you?*"

I could only blink in shock and stagger backward, pulling free of her chilled hands. My aunt *knew.* But how? How could she know the secret that had been only between my mother and me? Even my father had been unaware....

"What makes you say such a thing?" my mother asked gently. "How can you accuse your own sister?"

"Sister-in-law and not by blood," Matilda reminded my mother. "And I know. I've always been suspicious of you and your Pagan ways, Lily. From the time you helped me birth my firstborn and somehow took away the pain. And later, when you nursed me through the influenza that should have killed me. You with your herbs and brews." She waved a hand at the drying herbs that hung upside down in bunches from our walls, and at the jars filled with philters and powders, lining the roughly hewn wooden shelves. "No physician could ease my suffering the way you did." She said it unkindly, made it an accusation.

Slowly my mother nodded, her serene expression never

changing. "Herbs and plants are given by God, Matilda. Knowing how to use His gifts can surely be no sin."

"I saw you last full moon."

The words lay there, dropped like blows, as we stared at one another, my mother and I, both remembering our ritual beneath the full moon, when we chanted sacred words 'round a balefire at midnight.

"I know you have...powers. And I don't care if they're sinful or not. Not now. I need you to help Johnny. If you didn't conjure this plague, then prove it. Cure him, Lily. If you refuse...." Her eyes narrowed, but she didn't finish.

"If I refuse, you'll do what, dear sister? Bear witness against me to the magistrate? See me tried for witchery?"

Matilda didn't answer. She didn't need to. I saw her answer in her eyes, and my mother saw it as well.

"You've no need of such threats," Mother told her. "All you had to do was ask for my help. I'll try my best for your son, just as I did for Jonathon. But witchery or no, I may not be strong enough to help him."

"If he dies, I vow, I'll see you hang!" Aunt Matilda lurched toward the plank door, tugging it open on its rawhide hinges. "Gather what you need and come at once. I must make haste back to his bedside."

She left us in a swirl of snow, not bothering to close the door. I went and shut out the weather, then stood for a long moment, my hand on the door. I had a terrible premonition that the events of the past few moments would somehow change our lives forever. I didn't know how, or why, but I felt it to my bones. Drawing a deep breath, I turned to face my mother. I knelt before her, taking her hands in mine, staring up into eyes as black as my own. "Don't go to him," I begged her. "You cannot help him any more than you could help Father. And when he passes, she'll blame you."

"He is my own nephew," she whispered. She tugged her

hands away, got to her feet, and began to make ready, taking sprigs of herbs from the dried bunches hanging on the wall, pouring a bit of this powder and a bit of that into her special cauldron. The one with the hand-painted red rose adorning its squat belly. She added steamy water from the larger cast-iron pot that hung in the fireplace to the brew.

"We should leave this village," I pleaded as I worked at her side, measuring, stirring, holding my hands above each concoction to push magical energy and healing light into it. "We should leave tonight, Mother. Our secret is known, and you've told me how dangerous that can be."

"I can't break my vows," she said. "You know that. When someone needs help, asks me for help, I am bound by oath and by blood to try. And try I will." She looked into my eyes. "You should pack a bag and go to London. Take the horse. Leave tonight. I'll send for you when—"

"I won't leave you to face this alone," I whispered, and I flung myself into her arms, stroking her raven hair, so like my own, though hers was knotted up in back while mine hung loose to my waist. "Don't ask me to, Mother."

Her mouth curved in the first smile I'd seen cross her lips since my father's death. "So strong," she said softly. "And always, so very stubborn. All right, then. Come, let us hasten to Johnny."

We quickly packed our potions and some crystals and candles into a bag, pulled our worn homespun cloaks over our heads and shoulders, and stepped out into the brutal winter's night.

But my cousin was dead before we even arrived at my aunt's house. And we were greeted by a wild-eyed woman who'd once claimed us as kin, and the group of citizens she'd roused from slumber, all bearing torches and shouting, "Arrest them! Arrest the witches!"

Cruel hands gripped my arms, even as I turned to flee.

Accusations rang out in the night, and people stood round watching as my mother and I were surrounded, and then dragged over the frozen mud of the rutted streets. I cried out to my neighbors, begging for help, but none was forthcoming. And my heart turned cold with fear. As cold as the wind-driven snow that wet my face.

'Twas a long walk, the longest walk of my life. The poor shacks of the village fell away behind us as we were pulled and pushed along, and we emerged onto the cobbled streets that ran between the fine homes of the wealthy in the neighboring town. At last we stood before the house of the magistrate himself, trembling in the icy wind while our accusers pounded upon his door.

The man emerged in his nightclothes after a time, looking rumpled and irritated. "What's all this?" he demanded, white whiskers twitching.

"Two witches!" shouted the man who gripped my mother's arms tightly. "The ones who brought this plague on us all, Honor."

The old man's eyes widened, then narrowed again as he perused us. Beyond him I could see the glow of a fire in a large hearth, and feel its heat on my face. I longed to go warm my hands by that fire. My fingers were already numb from the cold.

"What evidence have you against them?" the magistrate asked.

"The word of this one's own sister," said another, pointing at my mother.

"Matilda is not my sister," my mother said, her voice ever calm, despite the madness around her. I would never forget her face, beautiful and serene. Her eyes, so brave, no hint of fear in them. "She is the sister of my husband."

"Your husband who died of the plague!" the man cried out. "And now your nephew is taken as well."

"Many have been lost to the plague, sir. Surely you wouldn't accuse every bereaved family of witchery?"

The man glared at my mother. "Matilda St. James bears witness, Honor. She's seen them practicing their dark rites with her own eyes."

"'Tis a lie!" I shouted. "My aunt is maddened with grief! She knows not what she says!"

"Silence." The magistrate's command sent shivers down my spine. He stepped forward, glancing down at the woven sack my mother still clutched in her hands. "What have you there, woman?"

Mother lifted her chin, meeting his gaze. I could see the thoughts moving behind his eyes, the way he looked at us, judging us, though we were strangers to him.

"'Tis only some herbs," she said softly, "brewed in a tea."

"She lies," the man said. "Matilda St. James said this woman was bringing a potion to cure her young son. But she feared the witch would deliberately wait until it was too late to help the lad, and her fear proved true. A witch's brew lies in that sack, Honor. Nothing less, I vow."

"'Tis no potion nor brew," my mother told him. "'Tis simply some medicinal tea, I tell you."

"Are you a physician, wench?" the magistrate demanded.

"You know that I am not."

"Give me the sack."

The hands holding my mother's arms eased their grip, and she gave her sack over. The magistrate opened it, pawing its contents, and I shuddered recalling the stones we'd put inside. Glittering amethyst and deep blue lapis, for healing. And the candles, made by our own hands and carved with magical symbols to aid in Johnny's recovery. We would have set them around his bed, where they would have burned all night to protect him from the ravages of the plague.

The magistrate saw all of this, and when he looked up

again, his eyes had gone cold. So cold I felt even more chilled despite the warmth from the fire at his back. "Put them in the stocks. We try them on the morrow. Perhaps a night in the square will convince them to confess and save us the time." He withdrew, leaving the door wide, and reappeared a moment later with a large key, which he handed over to one of the men. "See to it."

"No!" I cried. "You mustn't do this! We've done nothing wrong. Magistrate, please, I beg of you—"

His door closed on my pleas, and again I was pulled and dragged as I fought my captors. But my struggles were to no avail. And soon I found myself being forced to bend forward, my wrists and my neck pressed awkwardly into the stock's evil embrace. The heavy, wooden top piece was lowered as my own neighbors held me fast, and I heard the chain and the lock snapping tight.

I could not move. Could not see my mother, but I knew she was nearby, for I heard her voice, strained now, but steady. "Tell the magistrate he shall have my confession," she said. "But only if he will let my daughter go free. She knows nothing of this matter. Nothing at all. You must tell him."

The man to whom she spoke only grunted in reply. And then the villagers left us. In the town square, bent and held fast, we waited in silence for the dawn. The freezing wind cut like a razor, and the wet snow continued to slash at us. I shivered and began to cry, my face stinging with cold, my hands numb with it, my feet throbbing and swelling.

And then I heard my mother's gentle voice, chanting softly, "Sacred North wind, do us no harm. Ancient South wind, come, keep us warm." Over and over she repeated the words, and I forced my teeth to stop chattering and joined with her, closing my eyes and calling to the winds for aid. My mother's folk magic could not make iron chains melt away. But she could invoke the elements to do our bidding.

Within minutes the harsh wind gentled, and the snow stopped falling. A warmer breeze came to replace the bitter cold, and my shivering eased. I was still far from comfortable, bent this way, unable to relieve the ache in my back. But I knew my mother must be suffering far more than I, for her body was older than mine. Yet she did not complain. I took strength from that, and vowed to keep my discomfort to myself.

"Hard times await us, my daughter," she told me. "But whatever happens tomorrow, Raven, you must remember what I tell you now. Promise me you will."

"I promise," I whispered. "But, Mother, you mustn't confess anything to them. Not even to save me. I couldn't live if you were to die." The thought terrified me, and I pulled my hands against the rough wood that held them prisoner, though I could not hope to work them free. She was all I had in this world. All I had.

"Perhaps this is my destiny," she said softly. "But 'tis not yours."

"How can you know that?"

"I know," she whispered. "I've known from the day you were born, child. By the birthmark you bear upon your right hip. The crescent." Tears burned my eyes. But my mother went on. "You're a far more powerful witch than I have ever been, Raven."

"No. 'Tis not true. I can barely cast a decent circle."

She laughed then, softly, and the sound of it touched my heart. That she could laugh at a time like this only made me love and respect her more than I already did, though I'd never have thought it possible.

"I speak not of the form of ritual, but the force, Raven. The power is strong in you. And you will need that strength. When this is over, child, you must leave here. Go to the New World. My sister, Eleanor, is there, in a township called

Sanctuary, in the colony of Massachusetts. She is not a witch, and knows nothing of our ways. She was born of my father's faithlessness and raised by her own mother and not in our household. But she is kind. She will not turn you away."

"Perhaps not," I said. "But *I* will not leave you behind."

"I fear 'tis I who will leave you behind, my darling. 'Tis the night of the dark moon, when our powers ebb low. But even were our lady of the moon shining her full light down upon us, I doubt I could save myself. Do not cry for me, Raven. Dying is part of living, a birth into a new life. You know this."

"Oh, Mother, stop saying such things!" I cried loudly, sobbing and choking on my tears.

When Mother spoke again, I could hear tears in her voice as well. "Raven, listen to me. You must listen."

I tried to quiet myself, to do as she wished, but I vowed she would not die tomorrow. Somehow I would save her.

"When 'tis over," she told me, "you must return to our cottage in the village. But do so by night, and be very careful. You mustn't be seen. Do not wait too long, child, lest they burn the house in their vengeance or award it to Matilda's family in return for her testimony against us. You must go back in secret. Gather only what you will need for your journey. Then go to the hearth. There is a loose stone there. Take what you find hidden beyond that stone."

"But, Mother—"

"And take the horse, if she is still there. You may sell her in some other village. But take care. Should you meet anyone, do not tell them your true name. And as soon as you can, book passage on a ship to the New World. Now promise me you will do these things."

"I'll not let them kill you, Mother."

"There is nothing you can do to prevent it, child. I'll have your promise, though, and I will die in peace because of it. Promise me, Raven."

Sniffling, I muttered, "I promise."

"Good." She sighed, so deeply it seemed as if some great burden had been lifted from her shoulders. "Good," she whispered once more, and then she rested. Slept, perhaps. I could not be sure. I cried in silence from then on, not wishing to trouble my Mother with my tears. But I think she knew.

When dawn came, it brought with it the magistrate, and beside him a woman, looking distraught with red-rimmed eyes. Behind them walked a man who wore the robes of a priest. He had an aged face, thin and harsh, with a hooked nose that made me think of a hawk, or some other hungering bird of prey. He was pale, as if he were ill, or weak. And then they came closer, and I could see only their feet, for I could not tip my head back enough to see more.

"Lily St. James," the Magistrate said, "you and your daughter are charged with the crime of witchcraft. Will you confess to your crimes?"

My mother's voice was weaker now, and I could hear the pain in it. "I will confess only if you release my daughter. She is guilty of nothing."

"No," the woman said in a shrill voice. "You must execute them now, Hiram. Both of them!"

"But the law—" he began.

"The law! What care do you have for the law when our own child has become ill overnight? What more proof do you need?"

At her words my heart fell. She blamed us for her child's illness, just as my aunt had done. No one could save us now.

I heard footsteps then, and sensed the magistrate had gone closer to my mother. Leaning over her, he said, "Lift this curse, woman. Lift it now, I beg of you."

"I have brought no curse upon you, nor your family, sir," my mother told him. "Were it in my power to help your child, I would gladly do so. As I would have for my own husband and for my nephew. But I cannot."

"Execute them!" his wife shouted. "Michael was fine until you arrested these two! They brought this curse on him, made him ill out of pure vengeance, I tell you, and if they live long enough to kill him, they will! Execute them, husband. 'Tis the only way to save our son!"

The priest stepped forward then, his black robes hanging heavily about his feet and dragging through the wet snow. His steps were slow, as if they cost him a great effort. He went first to my mother, saying nothing, and I could not see what he did. But he came seconds later to me and closed his hand briefly around mine.

A surge of something, a crackling, shocking sensation jolted my hand and sizzled into my forearm, startling me so that I cried out.

"Do not harm my daughter!" my mother shouted.

The priest took his hand away, and the odd sensation vanished with his touch, leaving me shaken and confused. What had it been?

"I fear you are right," the priest said to the magistrate and his wife. "They must die, or your son surely will. And I fear there is no time for a trial. But God will forgive you that."

Pacing away, his back to us, the magistrate muttered, "Then I have little choice." And the three of them left us alone again. But only for a few brief moments.

"Mother," I whispered. "I'm so afraid."

"You've nothing to fear from them, Raven."

But I *did* fear. I'd never *felt* such fear grip me as I felt then, for within moments the priest had returned, and he brought several others with him. Large, strong men. People filled the streets as my mother and I were taken from the stocks. The people shouted and called us murderers and more. They threw things at us. Refuse and rotten food, even as the men bound our hands behind our backs and tossed us onto a rickety wagon, pulled by a single horse. I crawled close to my mother, where she sat straight and proud in that wagon, and I leaned against her, my head on her shoulder, my arms straining at their bonds, but unable to embrace her.

"Be strong," she told me. "Be brave, Raven. Don't let them see you tremble in fear before them."

"I am trying," I whispered.

The wagon drew to a stop, and the ride had been all too short. I looked up to see a gallows, one used so often it looked to be a permanent fixture here. I was dragged from the wagon, and my mother behind me. But she didn't fight as I did. She got to her feet and held her head high, and no one needed to force her up the wood steps to the platform, while I kicked and bit and thrashed against the hands of my captors.

She paused on those steps and looked back at me, caught my eyes, and sent a silent message. *Dignity.* She mouthed the word. And I stopped fighting. I tried to emulate her courage, her dignity, as I was marched up the steps to stand beside her, beneath a dangling noose. Someone lowered the rough rope around my neck and pulled it tight, and I struggled to be brave and strong, as she'd so often told me I was. But I knew I was trembling visibly, despite the warmth of the morning sun on my back, and I could not stop my tears.

That priest whose touch had so jolted me stood on the platform as well, old and stern-faced, his eyes all but gleaming beneath their film of ill health as he stared at me...as if in anticipation. Beside him stood another man who also wore the robes of clergy. This one was very young, my age, or perhaps a few years my elder. In his eyes there was no eagerness, no joy. Only horror, pure and undisguised. They were brown, his eyes, and they met mine and held them. I stared back at him, and he didn't look away, but held my gaze, searching my eyes while his own registered surprise, confusion. I felt something indescribable pass between us. Something that had no place here, amid this violence and hatred. It was as if we touched, but did so without touching. A feeling of warmth flowed between him and me, one so real it was almost palpable. And I knew he felt it, too, by the slight widening of his eyes.

Then his gaze broke away as he turned to the older man and said, "Nathanial, surely 'tis no way to serve the Lord."

The kiss of Scotland whispered through his voice.

"You are young, Brother Duncan," the older man said. "And this no doubt seems harsh to you."

"What it seems like to me, Father Dearborne, is murder."

"'Thou shalt not suffer a witch to live,'" the priest quoted.

"'Thou shalt not kill,'" the young Scot—Duncan—replied. And he looked at me again. "They've nay been tried."

"They were tried in the square by the magistrate himself."

"It canna be legal."

"His Honor's own child is ill with the plague. Would you have us wait for the child to die?"

The young man's gaze roamed my face, though he spoke to the old one. I felt the touch of those eyes as surely as if he caressed me with his gentle hands, instead of just his gaze.

"I would have us show mercy," he said softly. "We've no proof these women have brought the plague."

"And no proof they haven't. Why take the risk? They are only witches."

The beautiful man looked at the older one sharply. "They are human creatures just as we are, Nathanial." And he shook his head sadly. "What are their names?"

"Their names are unfit for a man of the cloth to utter. If you so pity them, Duncan, ease your conscience by praying for their souls. For what good it might do."

"'Tis wrong," Duncan declared urgently. "I'm sorry,

Father, but I canna be party to this."

"Then leave, Duncan Wallace!" The priest thrust out a gnarled finger, pointing to the steps.

Duncan hurried toward them, but he paused as he passed close to me. Then turned to face me, as if drawn by some unseen force. His hand rose, hesitated, then touched my hair, smoothing it away from my forehead. His thumb rubbed softly o'er my cheek, absorbing the moisture there. "Could I help you, mistress, believe me I would."

"Should you try they would only kill you, as well." My voice trembled as I spoke. "I beg you...Duncan...." His eyes shot to mine when I spoke his name, and I think he caught his breath. "Do not surrender your life in vain."

He looked at me so intently it was as if he searched my very soul, and I thought I glimpsed a shimmer of tears in his eyes.

"I willna forget you," he whispered, then shook his head, blinked, and continued, "in my prayers."

"If there be memory in death, Duncan Wallace," I said, speaking plainly, even boldly, for what had I to lose now? "I shall remember you always."

He drew his fingertips across my cheek, and suddenly leaned close and pressed his lips to my forehead. Then he moved on, his black robes rustling as he hurried down the steps.

"Do you wish to confess your sins and beg the Lord's forgiveness?" the old priest asked my mother.

I saw her lift her chin. "'Tis you who ought to be begging your god's forgiveness, sir. Not I."

The priest glared at her, then turned to me. "And you?"

"I have done nothing wrong," I said loudly. "My soul is far less stained than the soul of one who would hang an innocent and claim to do it in the name of God." Then I looked down at the crowd below us. "And far less stained than the souls of those who would turn out to watch murder being done!"

The crowd of spectators went silent, and I saw Duncan stop in his tracks there on the ground below us. He turned slowly, looking up and straight into my eyes. "Nay," he said, his voice firm. "'Tis wrong, an' I willna allow it!" Then suddenly he lunged forward, toward the steps again. But the guard at the bottom caught him in burly arms and flung him to the ground. A crowd closed around him as he tried to get up, and he was blocked from my view. I prayed they would not harm him.

"Be damned, then," the old priest said, and he turned away.

The hangman came to place a hood over my mother's head, but she flinched away from it. "Look upon my face as you kill me, if you have the courage."

Snarling, the man tossed the hood to the floor and never offered one to me. He took his spot by the lever that would end our lives. And I looked below again to see Duncan there, struggling while three large men held him fast. I had no idea what he thought he could do to prevent our deaths, but it was obvious he'd tried. Was still trying.

"'Tis wrong! Dinna do this thing, Nathanial!" he shouted over and over, but his words fell on deaf ears.

"Take heart," my mother whispered. "You will see him again. And know this, my darling. I love you."

I turned to meet her loving eyes. And then the floor fell away from beneath my feet, and I plunged through it. I heard Duncan's anguished cry. Then the rope reached its end, and there was a sudden painful snap in my neck that made my head explode and my vision turn red. And then no more. Only darkness.

Look for *Eternity*.

ALSO BY MAGGIE SHAYNE

Find more of Maggie's low-priced FUN-SIZED READS at maggieshayne.com/99.

Witch Moon

Magic By Moonlight

Everything She Does is Magic

Zombies! A Love Story

Spellbound

Sign up for Maggie's email updates so you never miss a freebie or bargain! Links to 6 FREE books with your first update. Visit maggieshayne.com/subscribe

ABOUT THE AUTHOR

New York Times bestselling author Maggie Shayne has published more than 50 novels and 23 novellas. She has written for 7 publishers and 2 soap operas, has racked up 15 Rita Award nominations and actually, finally, won the damn thing in 2005.

Maggie lives in a beautiful, century old, happily haunted farmhouse named "Serenity" in the wildest wilds of Cortland County, NY, with her soul-mate, Lance. They share a pair of English Mastiffs, Dozer & Daisy, and a little English Bulldog, Niblet, and the wise guardian and guru of them all, the feline Glory, who keeps the dogs firmly in their places. Maggie's a Wiccan high priestess (legal clergy even) and an avid follower of the Law of Attraction

Find Maggie at http://maggieshayne.com

Manufactured by Amazon.ca
Bolton, ON

13794479R00067